ONYE KINGSLEY
UNTOLD STORIES

kingsley onye
KINGSLEYBOOKS(UK) Ltd Ltd
Email: kingsleynonye@yahoo.com

D1783944

ISBN: 978-9988-2-6528-1

First Published by:
KINGSLEY PUBLISHERS
KINGSLEY BOOKS (UK) LTD.
WWW.KINGSLEYBOOKS.CO.UK
COPYRIGHT (C) 2018

Cover design and typesetting by:
Hetura Books Company (Ghana) Limited
+233-307-001-724
Website: www.heturabooks.com
Email: info@heturabooks.com

*Dedicated to the Millions of Hard
Working Health
And Social Care Workers saving lives
Around the World!*

INSPIRED BY A TRUE LIFE STORY

This novel is a work of fiction. Names, characters, places, and incidents are either a product of the author's imagination or are used ficticiously. Any resemblance to actual place, people living or dead, events or locales is entirely coincidental.

This is dedicated to the hard-working health and social care workers saving lives all over the world.

To the memory of ANTHONY NEWS; in whose benevolent mind building a home for vulnerable people was first conceived and who, with a determination undeterred by adverse circumstances, finally realised his dream. He came to live in this home after the death of his wife but died on 17th April, 1900.

"High Street Care Home Multipurpose" is dedicated in perpetuity to the glory of God and is founded by the Goodwill, Benevolent & District Housing Society Ltd, for the express purpose of serving those with dementia, mental health rehabilitation, learning disabilities, and young and elderly people of moderate means who are in need of accommodation in congenial and happy conditions where they may spend the evening of their lives.

If this is not a place where tears are understood.

Where do I go to cry?

If this is not a place where my spirit can take wing.

Where do I go to fly?

If this is not a place where my questions can be asked.

Where do I go to seek?

If this is not a place where my feelings can be heard.

Where do I go to speak?

If this is not a place where you will accept me as I am.

Where can I go to be?

If this is not a place where I can try to learn and grow.

Where do I just be me?

- William J. Crockett

FOREWORD

Untold Stories... clearly shows the challenges, prejudice, and laughter along with sadness and the need for "quality care" as well as the much needed investment for staff training, stringent monitoring of care, and a much needed change in legislation. A great powerful read that gripped me from the time I picked up the book.

-Beverley Hickey (one of the pioneers of "We Care" Networking Group and "Purple Angel Ambassador")

ACKNOWLEDGEMENT

I wish to acknowledge Jenny DeSouza, Pippa Taylor, Maureen, Ifeanyi (Jnr), Valentina, David, Martina, and Jackie Zvoushe for your support in my writing and publishing this novel.

I also say thank you to the team at Hetura Books for the editing, cover design, and typesetting work done.

Whoever contributed in any way to make this work a success, I say, thank you.

CONTENTS

CHAPTER ONE

AMANDA

"Good morning, Amanda," Frank greeted as he gently rapped at her door to ask after her wellbeing and provide her with support and care as he did at the beginning of each new day. But there was no reply.

He knocked again, waited for a reply but there was none. Now worried, he used the master key to unlock the door and entered the room. Amanda was already seated in front of her dressing table with her back to the door, peering in the mirror.

"Good morning, Amanda," repeated Frank.

"What do you know about a good morning?" she blurted out. Fuming in anger, she continued, "What do you know about someone being stuck in here 24/7, day after day, waiting to be sorted out by you lot? What do you know about good morning when everything is being done for you by total strangers? What do you know about having your freedom of choice, independence, dignity and respect being systematically eroded daily by people you don't know?

"Yes! You lot promised freedom and independence; we can see that now; can't we?" she answered sarcastically. "I mean... that is taken away from us every day under your overused slogan.... 'We owe you a duty of care; don't do this; don't do that; that's not good for you; we're acting in your best interests and that's not in your best interest; that's not in your care plan; your GP said this; your GP said that'," she mimicked stretching her neck towards Frank and mocking him as she derided the system.

"Yes! Tell me more," she continued. "Just go!" she cried in a melancholic voice with a twitchy note of a woman struggling so hard not to show her tears and give her enemy the victory of satisfaction.

"Leeeeeave meeeee alone!" she cried, now louder, almost hysterical.

It was a great deal for Frank to take in. He decided to give Amanda some space but resolved to approach her again when she calmed down. He left her room and closed the door quietly behind him; indicating that he wasn't angry at her outburst. In the meantime, he had to attend to other residents' needs with support from other duty staff according to the day's shift plan.

Frank Priye was a carer who loved his job. He worked with various care home organisations as agency staff and was often sent to different homes as a temporary care worker. Back home in Togo, West

Africa, he had a cousin, Innocent Priye, who suffered mental health problems and learning disability. He needed around-the-clock care, but his family was very poor and often left him to his own devices.

Frank had decided to spend time to care for him but without sufficient financial support with poor and very expensive medical treatment, Innocent had died at the age of twelve. Apparently, Society had no tolerance for the disabled and often treated them like outcasts.

Having arrived in England, Frank was determined to learn more about people with various disabilities and how they could be supported and cared for. Thus, when an opportunity for training presented itself, he grasped it with both hands and had worked in this field ever since. As time went on, he had moved through the ranks but always saw himself as a carer, first and foremost.

Amanda Jackson, 80, was formerly a chartered accountant with Gombey Multinational Oil Company. She was more focused on her career than in starting a family of her own; neither she nor her husband particularly liked children. They chose to devote most of their time to enjoy their successful careers; he as a successful playwright.

Things went well for them until they both retired ten years earlier on their seventieth birthdays. In celebration, they spent a little fortune organising the occasion and inviting friends and family. Two days after the celebrations, they embarked on a cruise around the world. No expense was spared; aboard the ship they made friends, partied. Occasionally the ship would dock in a port where they could disembark, enjoy sightseeing and savour the culinary delights of the host country.

The trip lasted two months and that eventually took its toll on James Jackson whose health was poor even before the trip. He acted against his doctor's advice and on returning from the exhausting cruise, he was infected with Escherichia Coli, a species of rod-shaped, facultative, anaerobic bacteria found in the large intestine of animals, sometimes pathogenic. One of the numerous restaurants they visited was to blame.

A few days after their return, his body was discovered by their maid in one of their ten flamboyant bedrooms in their mansion. After his burial, Mrs Jackson never fully recovered from the shock of losing her husband. Her high stress levels eventually led to the onset of dementia. This caused her to wander around the big mansion and she often strayed outside the home putting, herself in extreme danger as she wandered onto the local motorway.

She became so difficult to manage that her family could not handle her. It was then decided that a suitable care home would serve her best interests. Hence, she was moved to join other residents with similar health issues. Occasionally, she would ask the staff to book a cab for her to visit the cemetery where her husband was buried.

Two hours later, Frank Priye showed up again to attend to Amanda. She had calmed down and seemed very friendly but occasionally flew into a blinding rage and Heaven help whichever carer was on hand.

She was given breakfast with her morning medication but when the issue of personal care was mentioned, she hit the roof, looking at Frank directly with both hands shaking and raised into the air.

"Here they come again!" she shouted. "All I wanted to do today was to put my feet up and just stay in my bed all day without any fucking shower, thank you very much! I don't need one but will you let me? Hell no!"

Tilting her neck to one side, she continued, "You have to tell me what to do all the time…."

"Amanda, please calm down!" Frank interjected.

"Oh! Now you want to lecture me!" she shouted. "I knew already; now you'll tell me it was all written in my care plan – Bollocks! Fucking Bollocks!! That's what it is and once again, you'll be dragging in your shitty policy and procedure. I'm not ignorant of my care plans. Certainly, I don't need you shoving it down my throat time and again.

"These days, one no longer has the right to change one's mind without going through all these silly meetings; care manager this, care co-ordinator that, social worker this, social worker that; they swarm everywhere like vermin. loads of contradictions," she continued. "Nothing I want or say about myself matters anymore...I'm fed up, I just want to die. Oh God! Put me out of this misery. I can't take it anymore..."

She finally let go as a stream of tears flowed down her tired, wrinkly cheeks.

Frank was calm and full of empathy. "It's okay, Amanda. We can give you a quick wash to freshen you up. Will that be alright, love?" Frank cajoled.

Her calmness and resignation allowed Frank to give her a quick wash. It was all done in few minutes and she was wheeled to join others in the T.V lounge.

As Frank left Amanda, he went straight to Muriel's door to check on her and read her care plan for the day. She was an old pensioner with many illnesses. In the house diary, it was noted that a doctor's appointment had been booked for her as she complained of urinary incontinence and the inability to sleep well. She suffered high blood pressure and was also diabetic. She never liked any discussion regarding appointments in hospitals or seeing the doctor; not to mention nurses whom she always referred to as, 'Vultures in Uniform'.

Years back, her only son, Gabriel, had died of bowel cancer at the Curtis General Hospital, London. She had refused to believe the coroner's verdict that her son's cause of death was a result of bowel cancer which had spread to other parts of the small and large intestines. She preferred to point accusing fingers at nurses and doctors as a more reassuring way of dealing with her loss. She claimed her son had died due to negligence and that all those who worked in the hospital in that area, as far as she was concerned, were to blame.

As soon as she saw Frank, she silently made the sign of the cross on her forehead, hoping that nothing would be mentioned about hospital or a doctor's appointment.

She was quick to reply, "Yes," when Frank asked if she'd had a good night's sleep but when the topic changed to her being reminded of her doctor's appointment, her countenance changed and she wished he would leave her room immediately.

"Please remember your doctor's appointment at 12 o'clock," he repeated. "Muriel, make sure you are ready; a member of staff will support you for the appointment."

Frank quietly left her room with his body language indicating to Muriel how serious he was about it. She hated it whenever she felt cornered; she got on well with Frank and would not ruin it by sticking to her guns. In her mind, she knew he was doing his job and had been very polite, talking to her - unlike other members of staff who would simply rub her nose in it, knowing full well how much she detested doctors and nurses, "after all they had done to my son," she often said.

Josephine Abel, another carer on duty, was to support Muriel to her doctor's appointment. At 12 o'clock, she got Muriel dressed and ready for the appointment.

Dr Alfred Izak, her specialist doctor, did not take kindly to lateness. For him, lateness was like a crime. "You have robbed others of their time with me," he often exclaimed to anyone who came in late for their appointment. Most of his patients knew that and always endeavoured to be punctual.

The house car was with the garage

undergoing repair works so they had to make the journey by a cab which Frank had already booked. It arrived and was waiting for Muriel. She was in a wheelchair and took longer to manoeuvre herself into the cab.

After she got in, Josephine helped to put the wheelchair into the boot of the cab and off they drove to the hospital. As soon as they arrived, Muriel started.

"Oh no," she grumbled. "All they do is pump you with drugs as if you are their guinea pig...forgetting they all have side effects which you suffer afterwards. Question them further and they'll tell you it's for your own good....specialists my foot!"
She was still grumbling in the car when Josephine interrupted, "Save your breath. Let's get there first and see him; then you can tell him all this."

Shockingly, Muriel kept quiet. She darted her eyes to meet Josephine's and whispered, "Shall I...?"

"Of course, you have to let him know how you feel and all. Maybe he can offer you another therapy," Josephine confirmed.

Muriel was wheeled to Dr Alfred's office. They arrived on time and took their waiting ticket; theirs was number four.

"What's for dinner tonight?" Muriel questioned, as they sat waiting for their turn.

"We'll find out when we get home," replied Josephine. They were soon in Dr Izak's office who examined Muriel and prescribed more medication and advised the use of some more sanitary pads for her incontinence.

"I understand your concerns, but you have to be on this medication for a while. We'll monitor the outcome and possibly review it at a later date. Do you understand?" Dr Izak asked.

"Yes, agreed," said an agitated Muriel half-heartedly.

"Your next appointment will be in two weeks' time."

Muriel ignored him this time; her mind was at war kicking against more medication and prescriptions. She thought, "How dare you give me more medication?"

Even though she protested inwardly, she could not utter a word; she didn't want to be rude. However, Josephine bore the brunt when they left the GP's office.

"You should have told him I don't like medication. Instead, you stood there like a mother penguin while he was busily killing me with drug prescriptions! Oh dear! I'm fed up with you bunch!"

Muriel was still going on and on when suddenly, the blaring of the ice-cream van brought her to a sudden jolt.

"I want some ice-cream; stop the bloody van and get me some!" she ordered Josephine, who had been taking all her insults with professional calm. She realise, however, that she had no money; even the taxi they took, was on the company's account which was paid monthly by the housing organization. She was not given any money to spend on the short trip to the hospital so she had a lot of explaining to do to Muriel before the situation got out of hand.

"Oh dear, Muriel, I'm afraid we've got no money here for your ice-cream. The only reason we were out was to see your doctor and that's done. When we get home, there is plenty of ice-cream in the refrigerator."

Looking at her with alarm and surprise as if she'd just been stung by a bee, Muriel raged, "That's bullshit! Get me some money now; I want some ice-cream and don't waste my fucking time or I won't be going to any fucking home with you!" she threatened.

Josephine had to put her foot down because nothing she said or did would work. They had been there before. She merely repeated what she had said, "We have no money here at the moment; there are ice-creams in the refrigerator back home. You'll have them when we get home. Now, let's hurry up and, see, our Taxi is here already."

They soon boarded the taxi - that saved the day.

"Where is Missus? Oh my God! Has anyone fed her today?" Muriel questioned as soon as she alighted. Missus was a rescued, abandoned cat she'd got from Battersea Cats and Dogs' Home; an organization that cared for stray cats and dogs. She was lucky to have her from the animal sanctuary and renamed her 'Missus' because she was, she said, "My best mate."

Ever since Missus had arrived at the home, she had never lacked anything. Muriel often provided her with the best of everything she could afford and rarely let her out of her sight.

"Yeah, Missus was fed before we left," replied Josephine.

"Come on, dear," Muriel coo-ed, picking the animal up from the floor and stroking her. She soon forgot all about the ice-cream she had craved.

CHAPTER TWO

MADAM LOVELINE

"Tell you what? I've got no money, no salaries for you lot this month!"

Facing all other service users watching the TV who cared to listen, with her hands in the air, she declared, "The recession is biting hard. You can all stuff it and go home now to starve, not my problem."

She opened her palms. "Ask the managing directors," Madam Loveline Cricket concluded, then stood up and left as she made her way to the second TV lounge reserved for non-cigarette-smoking residents. She preferred staying there being a non-smoker herself.

She was only a 63-year-old woman, a chartered accountant, who had been laid off during the global Recession. She had worked with a big offshore company as their chief accountant before the collapse of the organization and had been in charge of processing and payment of staff salaries.

The sudden redundancy had come as a total shock to her; she wasn't prepared for it, and had earlier invested heavily in shares, stocks and bonds which had crashed with devastating consequences - all her investments had been wiped off, leaving her with nothing to fall back on for her long years of service.

Not knowing how to pick up the pieces of her life to start again, the stress led to early dementia with mental and psychological breakdown. She never truly recovered. She was brought to the home by her family who could no longer look after her since they all held demanding jobs. Because she loved her job so much, she often recreated role play scenarios in the home without knowing it. Most residents were already used to her antics and merely watched.

She kept a pet - an African parrot she named Patience, which always chirped and made residents' lives difficult. There had been countless reports about her. The management of the home deliberated on what to do without upsetting the apple cart. They didn't want to add to her pain and resorted to dialogue and negotiation on matters concerning her pet.

On Sunday afternoon, she was visited by her beloved family; two daughters and three grandchildren – two teenage boys and a toddler - a baby girl cradled by her mother. She occasionally smiled at her grandma but never got too close; she clung to her mom and never let go.

As soon as her family arrived, Madame Loveline acted well and said all the right things. The visit was amazing. Staff couldn't tell the difference between Madam Loveline's twin personalities but as soon as her visitors left, she rapidly slipped back into her usual self.

"Oh, Ken!" She shouted the name of a care staff on duty. "Can you take me out for shopping after dinner?" she begged.

"What would you like to buy?" Ken asked. "It's none of your business," challenged Madam Loveline. "I'm only asking so that I will know where to take you for the shopping."

She remained silent and rudely ignored Ken who still insisted on knowing what she wanted to buy and where to take her to save a wasted journey. Eventually, he decided to keep quiet about the issue and gave her some space. "She will come around," he thought. "She always does."

After dinner, she looked at Ken and beckoned him to come closer. She playfully placed her right hand on his shoulder and asked him to come close. She then tactfully whispered, "It's just window shopping, darling, and outdoor coffee at the Costa Cafe near Wallington Train Station."

"Okay, that's alright. I will take you there after your evening medication but we won't stay long like the other day; promise?"

"Promise!" replied Madam Loveline. The deal sealed, she became happy.

CHAPTER THREE
MURDER RAP

"If you hit me once more, I'll give it back to you, work or no work. I don't care!" retorted Mary Coulsdon, a Jamaican support worker who was virtually made a punch bag by Adam Slater, a very challenging resident with Obsessive Compulsive Disorder (OCD) and paranoid schizophrenia. He could be reasonable when he didn't skip his medication but he often thought that someone was after him for mischief and would take no chances.

He saw Mary serving lunch to other residents and swiftly went to her and landed a few punches on her face. "Why did you put poison in my food?" he queried. "You want me dead, innit?" he shouted as he rained blows on her.

It could have been worse if Mary had not blocked some of them with the empty plates in her left hand and if other staff hadn't suddenly intervened.

Afterwards, he was still gunning for her and refused to have his dinner. Frank, the shift leader, had to call the local police to forcibly remove him temporarily from the the home. He was taken to the local police station to be interrogated and came up with the story that Mary had been trying constantly to murder him.

The police were earlier informed about his mental state and they soon realized that he had been skipping his medication according to records. He was eventually sectioned to a local psychiatric facility. A few months later, he was back in the home.

It was once reported that Adam beat up a fellow resident claiming the poor fellow was exposing his penis to him, soliciting for sex. He'd found his actions rude and offensive and a voice in his head ordered him to act.so he kicked his balls. He just wasn't going to be molested by anyone, not by Silas Jnr or anyone else.

After their fight was broken up, Adam threw a large oven dish across the dining room that shattered the window pane as it flew out onto the lawn. Splinters of shattered glass went everywhere but luckily, no one was injured.

When questioned why he'd thrown the dish, he merely crossed his legs, leant back against the wall and replied, "I don't throw dishes, I throw people."

With his hands still in his pocket, he left quietly with an air of nonchalance, leaving

Carol Magnum, the house manager, short of words on how to handle him.

Adam Slater loved to run errands for other service users who felt too lazy to pop out in the freezing winter conditions. He did their personal shopping - especially cigarettes.

He often insisted they pay some commission for whatever errand he ran for them. "Oh ! Don't expect me to weather that cold for nothing and if you don't like it, you can lump it, or get off your fucking bum and get them yourself!"

Some of the residents who ventured out, often turned back halfway. They couldn't stand the freezing cold (minus 20 degrees) even when suitably-clothed for the weather. The truth is, they secretly felt it was their clever way of inflicting subtle punishment on Adam, the house bully.

For him, his gain outweighed the pain because he called the shots on his price for such an errand; and the more terrible the weather, the more they would have to pay him. As a result, he was the only one in the house who was never short of cigarettes. By the time he had run errands, his pockets were already full of goodies.

"Adam! How are you doing?" shouted Ibrahim Sani, a carer who bumped into him at Tesco's.

"Can't complain," grimaced Adam, whose hands were full of different brands of cigarettes for residents.

Most of the time, staff didn't get involved in shopping affairs as the residents seemed quite happy with the situation and hardly ever complained. However, due to the controversy surrounding Adam, he rarely aroused pity from the others who saw him as the strong man of the house who was capable of anything.

Actually, even though he had his own fears and vulnerable side, he was the de facto strongman of the house and no one messed him about but neither did anyone draw closer to him for friendship.

Those who did were there for only one thing – protection from others but most especially from him. As a result of that general perception of him, he simply played it his own way to get care and attention from others.

At times, he pushed it to an uncomfortable level and caused everyone to be scared. He could inflict an injury on himself to create a scene; staff would have no choice than to call an ambulance to take him to hospital for admission which generally lasted for quite some weeks. He loved that; it was his way of getting attention.

"The nurses are good. I love their tender loving care," he gushed to one of the care home staff who called to visit him with a get-well card signed by staff and residents.

When asked about the cause of the accident, he simply replied, "It was an accident; that's all I can tell you and don't push me any further," he gently warned.

Adam spent two weeks in hospital and made the lives of staff and patients very difficult with his numerous antics. He was once caught smoking a cigarette in the ward and was reprimanded by a staff nurse. It was reported by a fellow patient who begged for anonymity for fear of what Adam would do to him if he found out who shopped him.

But Adam was soon tired of the hospital routine and demanded to be discharged immediately. His request was quickly granted and he was soon back in the care home where he belonged and everyone was happy to see him back. Obviously, they had missed his occasional tantrums and weird character but especially his cigarette shopping for the house.

CHAPTER FOUR

AT HOME WITH DENNIS ARTHUR

Dennis Arthur woke up one morning with a start; a stream of early, bright sunshine seeping through the gap in his curtains. He yawned and placed his left palm on his forehead to soothe his brow.

He soon realized that he had been sleeping on a sheetless bed, having kicked them to the wooden floor. He savoured the joy of his beautiful dreams, remembering Lola's promise about a visit to the seaside and a picnic.

Lola was his lifestyle development support worker. That would be another interesting day, he smiled to himself. "Kenny Dionne is on shift this morning," he pondered. "I will wait for him to come and sort out my personal care."

Dennis thought that Kenny had arrived early because he heard a voice that sounded like his; or maybe, he was sitting in the T.V. lounge. "He's hoping I won't be waking so early today; well, I've got a surprise for him! He's wrong because I'm up, alive, kicking and already waiting to be sorted!"

The last word Dennis shouted aloud with a wicked smile on his face and he punched the air.

Dennis Arthur was born with autism and severe learning disability. His parents, Dennis Snr and Jancy Arthur, had four normal kids, now grown up, who were junior siblings to Dennis. He was the darling of the family. Despite his problems, all attention was focused on him almost to the neglect of his other siblings who seemed to understand their brother's plight and tagged along, knowing he needed more support than they did.

Dennis never went to a proper school as a child because he wouldn't mix favourably with other kids whom he often beat up at the slightest provocation. He came across as a bully, very domineering, and territorial; he wouldn't allow others to play with his toys, theirs, or those in the playroom at school.

His parents received letters from the head teacher bearing the countless complaints of parents whose children had been bullied and sometimes beaten up. The head teacher strongly recommended that Dennis would be better off elsewhere. The school could no longer tolerate his bullish attitude.

Dennis was soon moved to a new school but it wasn't long before he had punched a fellow pupil in the face because he wouldn't share his chocolate bars with him. The parents of Luke Jackson, his new victim, were furious.They had never heard of or seen anyone brazenly bully their son like that. They took the matter up very seriously; the school, police, social services and the education authority were involved.

Dennis, 10, was subsequently banned from attending a normal school.until a new placement could be found where he could be properly managed.

He had to remain at home with his parents and siblings who had learned how not to get in his way, watching a lot of television though he never seemed to concentrate on anything. He would put everything in a straight line, always matching colours and sizes, and could be seen, at times, idling about the house while his siblings were off to school.

His father owned a confectionery and household equipment shop across the road from their home. Occasionally, his mom would take him to see his father at the shop to spend some time with him. Those visits soon stopped because he hit and kicked some of the customers he didn't like.

Dennis loved to carry his transistor radio which he often tuned without interest in any station at all but seemed to be keen to have something sensory handy that produced sound. It seemed to calm him in spite of the constant and endless tuning in and out of stations.

One fateful morning, the postman made his rounds to their house to drop off mail. Dennis was squatting at the door entrance, tuning his radio as usual, when the postman arrived with a registered parcel that needed signing for.

As soon as Dennis caught sight of him, he stood up. The postman thought he was in luck to have found someone at home to give a signature. However, as soon as he got closer, Dennis grabbed him

tightly by his neck, threw him to the ground and rained blows on him. He tore his uniform and hit him repeatedly until the man cried out loud for help.

Fortunately, his mom and little sister were at home in the kitchen making breakfast. They came to the postman's rescue but only after he had received the beating of his life with minor cuts and bruises to his shoulders.

For Dennis, the postman's presence was an unwelcome intrusion into his privacy;

hence the attack. The incident was reported to the police and Dennis spent the night locked in the police cell. The matter went to court and he was eventually sectioned for six months at the young offenders' unit in Hounslow.

By the time he was set free, a rehabilitation home had already been found for him. He missed his father who only visited fortnightly. His siblings also visited from time to time.

And so it was that Adam Slater and Dennis Arthur found themselves living in the same care home. They didn't get on well ; each thinking he was stronger than the other. Staff and residents were happier when one of them was out of the house visiting their family for a few weeks or on holiday.

The secret rule was to never take your eyes off either of them when both were in the house, especially in the living room where all converged to watch TV or in the dining section during meal times.

Staff were instructed to mind them exclusively because failure to do so was often met with dire consequences; a possible blood bath and carnage. Neither of them would hesitate to use any dangerous object to attack the other nor indeed anyone else who stood in their way.

On one occasion,four residents and two staff were hospitalised for over a week with injuries sustained during the scuffle when they had clashed. That incident had been triggered by a simple disagreement over who sat where.

The most minor argument was enough reason for a serious scuffle. Very few care homes would dare take them on due to their poor record and the level of care and challenges they demanded.

Dennis loved his radio and would not have anyone tell him to turn down the volume - especially if he was not too happy on the day. The only one who dared was Frank, his key-worker, who he seemed to trust more than anyone else in the house.

Frank had supported him on several holidays and most outings and seemed to have a special bond and way of talking to him to get results. He often succeeded but at times they clashed if Dennis's bad mood got the better of him. Frank seemed to read the body language and made early retreat before Dennis kicked off. That way, he could still keep his hold and control in order to manage him.

✶✶✶✶✶

"Where is my ciggie?" Amanda demanded.

Adam fumbled in his trouser pocket and brought out a half packet of Benson & Hedges and handed it to her.

"I gave you money for a full packet! How dare you open my packet of cigarettes?" she snapped.

"Then how do I get my commission for the errand?" Adam retorted. "Also, remember the same shit happened yesterday. You find it difficult to pay commission on errands; next time remember to nip out yourself to buy your fucking cigarette," he went on. "You are now officially off my fucking list!" Pointing at her, he shouted, "Got that?"

A bewildered Amanda simply ignored him focusing instead on lighting her cigarette. She inhaled deeply, then blew out long spirals of smoke and seemed very satisfied with herself as she murmured, "Whatever! Anyway, how's the weather out there? Terribly cold, isn't it?"

She looked up at Dennis for affirmation; he seemed more engrossed with tuning his radio while Adam interjected, emphasizing, "See why you need to pay me more commission then?"

He turned to her, leaning towards her with his cigarette, wanting a light from hers.

"Ummh whatever," replied Amanda.

Dennis didn't smoke but often picked up the butts to play with them. As soon as a butt was thrown on the floor, he rushed for it. On one occasion he picked up a smouldering cigarette and got his fingers burnt and forbade anyone to talk about it.

Dennis occasionally liked to make trips by public transport on his own, but due to constant reports by members of the public who he beat up or harassed, a new care plan was fashioned for him - he was to be accompanied on outings by a one-to-one escort, a member of staff to monitor and curb his excesses.

Frank opted to escort him on public transport from Coulsdon to Mitcham Junction, a journey of a few hours by bus. He always carried his disabled badge and a free travel card which he was entitled to.

As soon as they stepped onto the bus, Dennis started at the top of his voice, "Hey everybody! This is my carer, his name is Frank and he is a good nurse......"

He was still talking instead of finding himself a seat and settling down. He suffered poor mobility as a result of conditions he endured as a child. He had never met any of the passengers before, yet he talked to them with all the familiarity of a bosom friend.

When he eventually searched for a seat, after ignoring Frank's advice to do so from the start, he found that they were all occupied.

Frank actually preferred to stand. However, as the bus negotiated a sharp curve, Dennis grabbed at a lady to avoid falling over. As the bus stabilized, he marched up to a woman sitting close to the driver and ordered, "Don't you know you should stand up for me because I am disabled?"

Before the woman could reply, Dennis started pushing her off her seat. A massive row erupted and the driver had to stop the bus and ordered Dennis to leave the bus immediately.

Fortunately, Frank's sudden intervention saved the day but as soon as the bus started moving again, Dennis looked at the woman with a disgusted look on his face and blurted out, "You foolish woman!"

At this point ,the poor woman decided enough was enough. She demanded the address of the care home and a few weeks later, a letter was received addressed to the manager reporting the incident on the bus. The woman threatened to take the matter further unless Dennis sent a letter within a week apologizing for his crude behaviour.

The letter was read to Dennis in the manager's office with Frank present. It was made clear to Dennis that he must apologize. He grudgingly agreed and was given a plain sheet of paper to write his reply. After some struggle, he scribbled some muddled up words but the intention was clear and visible,

'I'm deeply sorry for offending you. Don't know how the devil got into me; please forgive me. It will not happen again," signed and dated – Dennis Arthur.

Frank helped him to post the letter and that seemed to put a closure to the incident.

CHAPTER FIVE

EVELYN NORMANDY

Evelyn Normandy was a 20-year-old lady with paranoid schizophrenia, such a lovely soul when her mood was stable but chaotic and anarchic when she wasn't. This usually happened when she was determined not to follow her medication regime which, thankfully, did not happen often.

Behind the bravado was an angel with a beautiful soul. She was released from a higher support system to a lower one and lived in a supported residential home just across the road from the other care home in the next street.

She knew that if she behaved herself and abided by her daily medication, she should be fine. The problem was that the spirit was willing but the body was weak. She always dreamed of having her own flat to live in, with very minimal support or none at all, but she knew she had to earn it.

When she was 15 and still living at home, her uncle, Kevin, visited London, where she lived, from Manchester. He often arrived with the excuse of not staying in an hotel, when he could easily stay with his brother (Evelyn's father) and save costs.

Evelyn's mother had died in an expedition mishap some years back and Evelyn had been brought up solely by her father and a few family members. Uncle Kevin started buying her expensive presents and then occasionally touching her inappropriately.

Initially, she thought nothing of it until one fateful night. Her father, a plumber by trade, was away in Dublin fixing a client's drainage, leaving her behind with Uncle Kevin. After dinner, Evelyn retired to her room for the night to do some knitting which was one of her hobbies.

She enjoyed knitting and it helped to keep her busy when no-one was around since her father travelled a lot. In fact, her knitting project at the time was a large sweater, a secret birthday present for her father's fifty-fifth birthday which was soon going to be celebrated at home.

Evelyn had invited family and friends to grace the occasion; a surprise party. The problem was finding a way to get her father to stay at home for the celebration. Even so, she had a plan - she would take all his work tool boxes out of his mini-van and hide them!

She smiled to herself, thinking it over as she drifted off to sleep.

Kevin was busy idling away in the lounge downstairs, watching TV.

But in the middle of the night when she was deeply asleep, a shadowy figure of a man crept soundlessly into Evelyn's room. He lingered for a moment in the doorway before moving slowly towards the bed, cursing quietly under his breath as his knee knocked against the frame.

He steadied himself, then focused on the sound of the young woman's quiet, steady, rhythmic breaths. Such was his increasing excitement and anticipation that he was acutely unaware of the marked contrast to his own shallow, laboured breaths; his heart beating loudly in his over- heavy body.

He shuffled clumsily along the side of the bed in the dark and then stooped to run his hands along the edge of a heavy, woollen duvet. He lifted it a little, holding his breath as he did, and slowly edged himself onto the bed and under the covers beside his unsuspecting victim.

Now very close, he could smell the faint aroma of her perfume which only served to increase his raging desire for her. He had waited too long for that moment as he was tormented by her loveliness. His fat, clammy hands moved swiftly and found soft, warm, naked flesh.

Evelyn stirred slightly in her sleep as the groping hands moved quickly, searching, then finding her beautiful, firm, breasts. He cupped them momentarily in his hands, savouring the moment, before greedily moving down her body.

Suddenly, she was awake, wrenched away from her night slumber and struggling to comprehend what was happening to her. A split second later, fear and horror swapped places with innocent dreams. Her violator was on top of her now, cruelly bruising her with his roughness.

She was pinned to the bed, unable to move. She tried to scream but no sound was audible from her trembling mouth. Fear turned to terror when she realized his intentions. She was powerless to stop him. He paused briefly to fumble with his trouser buttons, then raped her brutally, pounding into her delicate body, again and again, bulldozing his way through her.

Despite the searing pain she was forced to endure, she somehow managed to free her arm from under his vile, labouring body and flailed around in desperation, reaching for something; anything that might serve as a weapon.

Momentarily, her fingers brushed the cold steel of her knitting needles. She reached again and found them, this time grasping them tightly in her fist with all the force she could muster. She rammed the makeshift weapon into his pulsating neck, fortuitously severing the carotid artery, stabbing wildly, again and again, with all her might.

She then went on a stabbing spree, poking it constantly and forcefully into every part of his body she could reach. She kept stabbing non-stop until she felt warm blood everywhere and was able to push off his lifeless body as he fell on the floor.

Fearfully, she jumped out of her bed and switched on the light. To her greatest shock, it was her uncle. With blood everywhere, she became so confused but tried to calm down, enough to call the ambulance.

Kevin had lost so much blood that he died in the ambulance half way to the hospital.

The police were also called and the murder case investigations began, followed by the coroner's report. The trauma of knowing that her trusted uncle could ever think of raping her sent her over the precipice of a negative emotional roller coaster from which she never seemed to truly recover.

Her case later went to the High Court where she pleaded diminished responsibility; that she had acted in self-defence as she had feared she would be murdered afterwards by her attacker. After careful consideration of the evidence and her circumstances, the judge charged her with the lesser offence of manslaughter. She was, however, sentenced to two years in a mental health institution with counselling and support for her trauma but the damage was already done. She ended up with paranoid schizophrenia by the time she had completed half of her sentence and she was sent to a lesser support unit where she was looked after.

As she gradually stabilized, she found herself living few metres away from Dennis and Adam. The residents of the care home often met at the city leisure centre for bowling and salsa dance lessons on Wednesdays and when Evelyn was there, her presence often gave the two men butterflies.

Before that, Adam had never seemed to like attending but it all changed when Evelyn joined in. Since then, he and Dennis had been in competition for her affection and couldn't afford to miss a session. The rivalry between them grew deeper with each passing day.

Whatever Dennis wanted, Adam also wanted and Evelyn seemed to be the apple of their eyes. Neither was ready to let go.

Interestingly, Evelyn was totally unaware of the dust her presence was gathering with the two men struggling for her attention. She couldn't care less; the trauma she'd been through was more than enough to scare her off men for a very long time to come.

Evelyn was still in the home when her father visited. He made a point of visiting monthly due to his difficult job schedule. Whenever he did, it was presents for everyone, especially his daughter whom he loved dearly because she was his constant reminder of his gorgeous late wife, Judith.

Judith had been an experienced mountain climber, as he was, too, but he had lost her during a Mount Everest climbing expedition that had gone wrong in the early 1980s. What had started as a lovely holiday in Nepal on the borders of Tibet and Nepal, the Himalayas and South Asia, ended up a nightmare.

Back in England several years later, on a beautiful, Easter day after the morning service, he drove all the way from Coventry to spend the

day with his daughter bearing a lot of Easter eggs among other things, new clothes, dressing gowns, wrist watch and shoes. He ensured that every resident received the present of an Easter egg.

While everyone was enjoying their chocolate, Dennis was busy cosying up to Miss Normandy, begging her to hand over hers. She

merely ignored him and strutted to sit beside Alan Sydney, who was only too pleased to have her company.

CHAPTER SIX

I AM NOT YOUR SLAVE

"You do it!" blasted Terry Gordon, one of the newly-admitted residents with mental health issues undergoing a rehabilitation programme. He was showing his anger and frustration on why he had to stamp out the smouldering stub of his recently-smoked cigarette, carelessly thrown on the carpet with a smouldering fragment of fire gradually eating up the new rug in the general lounge.

While James Blaster, the duty officer, was trying to encourage him to put out the stubs to avoid any fire disaster that could break out, Terry was more interested in pinching cigarettes, a different brand, that Adam had left on the centre table; a deliberate bait for troublemaking.

He often did this to cause chaos in the house and woe betide whoever pinched his cigarettes because even if you were lucky to survive his assault, you would be his errand slave for a long time to come. You would be indebted to him and naturally bound to do his dirty work like going shopping in the rain for others while he took the benefits or 'commission' as he often called it, or do his laundry. You would be at his beck and call until he found another victim.

Staff knew what was going on but didn't want to get involved knowing how dangerous some clients could be. "Stand in ma way; I'll just waste yah. Jury found me guilty; return me to strong room kepis! Big deal!" he often said.

By that, he meant prison or a mental health secure unit to start treatment all over again. He knew his life was up and down but couldn't care less about anyone who happened to be dragged in, one way or another.

As soon as Toby Bikinis picked up the cigarette, all eyes turned towards him as if some monster had just popped out from the graveyard. That made him wary and uncomfortable; almost in jitters.

He asked, "Whose cigarettes are those?"

"Adam's!" chorused everyone who had long been avoiding any form of contact with the cursed cigarettes as they often called them.

The mention of his name sent millions of electric volt shivers down his spine. Toby Bikins instantly dropped the cigarettes just exactly where he had picked them up.

He'd had a terrible encounter with Adam the previous week and was really lucky to have escaped because he had been pinned to the toilet wall for hours with a large pair of garden scissors across his throat with his neck in-between the open V-shaped, sharp-edged blade, just few inches grazing away from his neck and throat.

With two quick, sharp punches to his stomach to remind him not to mess with him again, Adam had strained his clenched teeth and mouth very close to Toby's ears and whispered, "You stepped on ma feet last week, dinner time, with no sorry. This is to remind yah never to fuck wiv me again okay?"

Toby had been too shocked to reply but he only struggled to nod his head in agreement before Adam convinced himself to let him go. That had happened at the back of the large garden fields by the toilet, a few metres away from the main house near the long tennis court and no one else had seen what happened. Adam had been very careful of that.

He warned, "Breathe a word of this to any soul and we'll be shopping for yah coffin; do yah understand?"

Toby Bikins was terribly shaken by the incident and never spoke a word of it to anyone. So the fact that the cigarette he picked up belonged to Adam meant he surely needed his own head re-examining or something.

"What was I finking?" he asked himself as he quickly left the large TV lounge with a rush to his bedroom's toilet. "At times I can't believe myself," he wondered again, as he pulled down his underpants to let loose a hot wee.

After a couple of minutes, Adam sauntered into the lounge and went straight for his cigarettes, still lying where he'd left them as bait. Everyone turned their eyes away and stared at the TV programme no

one was really interested in. There was total silence except for the noise coming from the refrigerators and washing machines adjacent to the house. Those who could not stand the heat and the tension of the moment simply disappeared quietly into their rooms.

Weeks later, Adam visited his G.P to complain about his deteriorating mental health. Sitting in front of his psychiatrist and with his right hand massaging his forehead, he blurted, "Doc, in my mind I feel like an open window curtain. Each time I wake up, I feel blank, not knowing what to do with myself in the morning."

"If you feel like an opened window, maybe it's time you pulled yourself together, close the curtains," his doctor joked, as he finally prescribed some medication for him which he took to his local pharmacy.

Frank Priye was to support Adam to pick up the prescriptions but Adam quickly left before Frank could join him and had to run to meet up with him. The pharmacy needed a detailed explanation and Frank had to collect other residents' weekly medication as well.

"Am I your slave?" blurted Adam, as Frank encouraged him to lend him a helping hand to move the little bulk of the medications so that they could put it on a trolley for easy transportation home.

"Of course you're not my slave and I am not yours either."

"No, you are mine because you work for me in my house," Adam retorted.

"Adam, I am only here to support and care for you till you get better and I get paid to do that; it's not for free and I also pay my tax which the government gives the council to pay for the services you use for your upkeep and services in the community," Frank explained.

"You see, you are my slave; you work for me in my house and cook my food and everything and guess what? I do nothing all day but eat, drink, wee, poo, smoke, watch TV and on weekends I get my pay packet all for doing nothing," Adam insisted, this time angrily.

Frank got the message. Adam was already worked up and very angry; to push that any further would not be a good idea, so he simply ignored him and changed the topic.

"How are preparations for your coming holiday?" he probed with a broad smile on his face.

"We are going to Shropshire; I can't wait," he added. "Frank, are you coming with us? Josephine is coming, too. We are going to make a BBQ there, swim and see the Mermaid"...he was so excited and went on and on without waiting to hear from Frank.

He was still talking when they rang the house bell. They were home and Adam was so happy that he was the one who eventually pushed

the medication trolley back home and seemed to have enjoyed doing that.

"Can I have a cigarette?" he begged Amanda who was in her wheelchair in the large lounge stroking Billy, her two-month-old dog, a Yorkshire Terrier, a gift from Thomas, her brother-in-law. She was also listening to the current news items on the T.V.

Adam's voice was a total unwelcome diversion. "What happened to the magic word, 'Please'? Have you lost your manners?" attacked Amanda, without even looking in his direction. She was the only one in the home who could stand up to Adam and call off his bluff. That often brought him to order; no one knew what powers she used to accomplish that.

Adam was quite mindful of her and she knew he was a nut-case, however she never overdid it, and knew when to step in to tell him off and when to keep a distance.

Adam had never really grown up with his mother as he was always in and out of hospitals and prisons. So, he saw Amanda as a mother figure to occasionally warm up to.

"Okay, please can I have a cigarette? I will pay you back, I promise," he asked again, now politely.

Without saying a word or looking at him, she flicked out a brand new packet of Benson & Hedges and tapped its bottom to push out a stick

for Adam which he hurriedly snatched and soon disappeared into the smoking lounge.

The smoking lounge was like a no-man's land. In that single room, people kept quiet, minded their own business and smoked in silence; at times stubbing out on the chairs, tables, and ash trays. The staff's complaints of health and safety often fell on deaf ears as most inhaled one another's second-hand smoke by not opening the windows to let it out; even the smoke extractors on the wall were often switched off by someone who hated its noise.

As a result, staff occasionally popped in there to open up shutters and switch on the extractors. The level of self-demotivation was so high that residents found excuses for not doing things at all to better themselves for the future; for them, life was all about eating, drinking, smoking ciggies and going the extra mile to manipulate the system.

"I fucking slashed a neighbour's throat and he was rushed to the hospital; he didn't make it. He died. They charged me wiv murder, sent me to prison for ten years, I served ma time, and they brought me here; they should have sent me home instead but papa and momma wouldn't have me back. In my mind I am still in prison," Adam reminisced, as he narrated his life story to Terry Gordon among others in the smoking room.

Andrew Jacob, a new black South African employee from the agency, entered the smoke-filled room to open up the place for fresh air as the usual house routine. As soon as Thomas Gaffe sighted him, he shouted, "You lot came in here flooding like vermin and vultures on a dead carcass, go back to your home country where you came from; we are fed up. Enough is enough!"

He was still shouting his racist rants when Andrew walked across the room and opened up the closed windows. Everyone knew Thomas as a very unfriendly man towards coloured people. He never saw eye to eye with foreigners; he thought they were only in England as rip-offs and should be sent straight away back to wherever they came from with a one-way ticket.

Several attempts had been made by the management to educate him on how to respect others and their cultural diversities but all attempts were futile. For him, he thought, "It's my duty to protect my country and none of you can shut me up. I speak my mind; no apologies," he concluded.

Andrew allowed him to finish and later returned to talk with him after dinner. "I hope you realise how offensive your words are; those are racist comments and I hope you realise that," Andrew explained.

"Yes, you heard me; go back to your country where you came from. We don't want you here," he shouted even louder to the surprise of everyone.

"Andrew, don't mind him," pleaded Amanda. She turned to Thomas, "In a few hours' time you should be ready for bed; your health is so poor as it stands now. You're all mouth, you can't walk, you can't jump, you could barely see, you've actually passed your sell-by date. Guess who will clean you up and tuck you in bed tonight?" she teased.

Thomas, who would be celebrating his 85th birthday the following week, replied, "Him of course," as he nodded in Andrew's direction.

"And what about your conscience?" Amanda queried. "Well, that one was dead long ago because there won't be any compromise with rip-offs and someone nipping off the boat and sneaking into my country," Thomas concluded.

"Then you'll be hopping mad if he wishes to withdraw his services tonight. I think I am looking at a man who might end up spending the rest of the night in his wheel-chair and that might teach him a lesson to show respect to others," Amanda chuckled as Andrew realised the fruitlessness of trying to make Thomas see sense.

Andrew merely recorded Thomas's rants in his daily book but no one ever seemed to have talked about it and everyone carried on as normal as possible as if it never happened. There was little or nothing the management would do about it. As things were, all that mattered was the profit coming in from the council for the services; anything outside that was of less importance.

"Andrew should know by now that is the part of the package of the job. He should take it like a man and soldier on and pay less attention to such issues," reiterated Carol Magnum, the house manager after reading Andrew's complaint.

With no emotional or psychological support for the staff, the issue went away quietly as if it had never happened, with Thomas showing no remorse for his actions.

"We go through this every day," noted Frank Priye, patting Andrew's shoulder. He advised, "Just do the job and go home, brother. In this job, we're nothing but doormats. Push this any further and you are schemed out of the job with flimsy excuses from the powers above; the bosses," he whispered.

Evelyn Normandy sat in the large TV lounge pretending to be watching the TV news item while eavesdropping on the conversation ensuing between Andrew Jacob and Frank Priye. At the end of it she coughed slightly to attract their attention. As they both looked in her direction, she said, "Don't worry, darling; your secrets are safe with me."She smile, got up and strolled through the corridor leading into the manager's office.

CHAPTER SEVEN

MURIEL'S CAT "Missus"

Missus seemed to get along with almost everyone in the home except a few people she chose to dislike. She couldn't stand Adam Slater and Dennis Arthur who occasionally harassed her by kicking her and often hiding away her silver plate and water cup in the darkened corners of the hallway.

Thankfully, if not for her sharp nose for smell, life would have been more difficult and each time that happened, she made it a duty to stroll into the T.V lounge where the culprits were and deliberately stand in front of them to give them a long hard look that sought to say, "Rude boys, the pair of you, keep off my food plate and water or else….."

As soon as she turned to leave, Adam and Dennis looked at each other with a wicked smile on their faces and suddenly, Missus looked back at them. Seeing their chuckle, she stared at them again as if saying, "You heard me, pig heads," and quickly disappeared into Muriel's room for safety.

They seemed to get the message and often kept away for few weeks or so before another torment would begin. However, Muriel got to know about Missus's plight and took the matter a bit further to register her disapproval of their actions; she stopped sending Adam to buy her ciggies. This meant some loss of commission in cash or kind.

Patience, Madam Loveline's African grey parrot, seemed to get along very well with

Missus even though she rarely left her grey-coloured cage on the balcony. She seemed to know every resident's name by heart; at times she reeled out a repertoire of names she in her memory bank when angry or desperate for attention. She did that so well that people left whatever they were doing and rushed towards the balcony only to realise they had been fooled.

The only people Patience didn't get along with were Adam and Dennis; no-one could figure out why until a member of staff caught Adam banging a spoon against her metal cage to scare her off as the poor bird kept chirping, "Fuck off, Adam! Adam, fuck off!! Adam, Adam, fuck off; fuck off!!!"

This went on for about three seconds until a member of staff intervened. They insisted that Adam apologise to Patience for his rudeness and harassment. After thinking for a long time, Adam drew close to her cage and muttered, "I am very sorry, Patience."

"Piss off, you idiot!"chirped Patience as she started hopping about in her cage in agitation. Adam shamefully walked away with thoughts in his mind.

Later in the day, Patience was brought to the house front passageway for few hours a day as usual. Muriel who did not believe in caging pets though she had to for the house rules. However, she often made sure she was there with Missus to prevent passersby making away with her precious pet.

For Patience, that was the best time to make more friends and luckily, acquire more goodies and collectibles; she never missed an opportunity to shriek, "Hello!" to anyone passing through; some would ignore her while others found her irresistible.

"Frank! Frank!! Frank!!!" she fluffed and ran riot in her cage. Muriel and others wondered what all the fuss was about until they looked further and saw Frank Priye just alighted from the bus and marching towards the house.

He was on a late shift that ran into a sleep-in; that was when everyone realised the reason for her agitation. She liked Frank like everyone else; with him, she knew she was in safe hands with lots of goodies on the way.

When less busy, occasionally, Frank brought her out of her cage for a short exercise and play session coupled with a little tender loving care as he ran his hands over her beautiful feathers. She loved it. The calm and look in her eyes told the tale.

As soon as Frank had exchanged pleasantries with Patience and Muriel, he entered the house and shut the door behind him.

"Here they come again," murmured Thomas Gaffe. "They are all over the place," he said without even looking in Frank's direction. Frank's greetings were met with deafening silence but he simply ignored that and went straight into the office for the handover session, wondering what the day's shift would look like as he took down notes.

CHAPTER EIGHT

HOUSE PARTY

It was the tenth anniversary of the home, residents and staff couldn't wait to grace the occasion. There would be lots to eat and drink. Everyone dressed their best, even Missus was given a bow-tie courtesy of Muriel who loved to show off what a good pet she had even though Missus found it awkward (a cat wearing a bow-tie!) but managed to keep her cool, not without giving her owner that look of, "What's the meaning of all this?" which her owner immediately ignored or rather buried in the excitement of the day.

Patience, the African grey parrot, was ringed with gold on her right foot which she carried with pride and was busy making enough noise to attract attention to herself to show off her new jewellery. It was suggested that they move her cage further down the back garden as her noise was almost drowning the music but there was a change of mind as she was also as a great part of the day's fun and visitors kept going up to her to offer her treats.

Terry Gordon, Adam Slater, Dennis Arthur, Amanda Jackson, Catherine Drizzler, Madam Loveline, Thomas Gaffe and others appeared in what looked like their best clothes as ensured by their various carers. Everyone was looking great; even the staff and management were looking fabulous. The meal was gorgeous; different dishes were on offer and one had to serve oneself.

Adam and Terry occasionally sneaked out for cigarette. Dennis and Adam seemed to be in a serious competition on who won Catherine's affection. Dennis pulled a fast one by changing his gait and tilting his body to his left in a somewhat stylish manner, matching it with a little limpy walk; occasionally putting his left hand in his pocket. Now and then he would stroke his red tie. He wasn't leaving anything to chance-he had been sleeplessly waiting for that moment to let Cathy know how much he fancied her.

Initially, concerned staff became worried thinking, he had had an accident or had something sticking under his heels but on closer examination, he was revealed to be fine and merely told staff in no uncertain terms to mind their own business and not to worry about him. As soon as they saw him heading towards Catherine with the same gait, they all realised what was on and merely minded their businesses though they kept a watchful distance to check that that both parties were okay.

Catherine was fully aware of the affection Dennis and Adam had for her but they couldn't tell her how they felt about her for fear of rejection. They seemed to clearly lack the confidence of doing that and were content to occasionally have her attention no matter how brief.

Staff saw Dennis giving her a handmade card; one of the few things he learned during one of the in-house art lessons on which he'd scrawled, 'Beautiful Cathy, signed, Dennis,' at the bottom. It was a wriggly drawing of a fluffy-haired lady wearing stiletto shoes with a flowery lady's handbag carrying a cat, presumably Missus.

Catherine collected it with a smile, opened it and chucked it in her bag and muttered, "Thank you."

Little did everyone know that Adam was watching; he too strolled towards her and offered her a packet of Benson & Hedges with a new green lighter. Catherine was surprised at the gift as a non-smoker. She merely laughed it off and refused the gift and said, "Thank you, but I am not a smoker."

"Try it," Adam suggested as she left to queue for her dinner while Dennis was still looking on and wondering what the hell Adam was telling her. Soon, he joined the dinner queue with a massive plate in his hands. Everything went quiet for a while except for the clanging and banging of cups, plates, and cutlery as everyone was having a mouthful of food.

Frank Priye had to serve Muriel her dinner and other residents with poor mobility. Muriel was sitting next to Peter, another service user. She was stroking Missus when Peter finished her dinner in three grabs of his hands. She couldn't stop him and when Frank and other staff realised what was happening, they approached Peter who had positioned his own food and was about to start eating.

He was promptly stopped and asked why he had eaten Muriel's food. Frank did not bother to hear all his waffling. He simply gave Peter's dinner to Muriel and instructed him to return to the T.V. lounge which he obeyed, knowing he was in the wrong.

Music was blaring from the loud-speakers of the hired DJ; it was the oldies' hit songs of the 70s, 80s, and 90s. Most of the residents were quite familiar with some of the songs and some simply sang along to the envy of others. Those who wouldn't sing along chose to jig along on the dance floor.

Even staff were not left out. Some joined the residents to dance and sing along and make merry. Adam and Catherine took to the dance floor to Dennis Arthur's amazement. He looked like a green-eyed monster. So he waited for a while and went to them and asked Adam to excuse him to allow him to dance with Catherine. But before he could oblige, Catherine had had enough and went to sit down to rest her feet.

Dennis didn't take kindly to that, believing that she loathed him and preferred Adam to him. As a result, he went grumpy, and refused to talk to anyone. At one point he was seen throwing plates and cutlery and had to be restrained before he caused further damage.

For Adam, the competition had just begun while Catherine was oblivious of the rift and tension around her. Staff had chosen to keep a close eye on both men; some even prayed not to be on shift that day, knowing the whole thing could blow up because no-one messed with those two men when they locked horns.

It usually took several truck loads of policemen to calm the situation. The last time they had clashed, many were hospitalised for weeks afterwards.

Eddy Wisdom, a retired British army officer from the Iraqi war, then one of the residents after suffering from a near fatal injury as a result of a land mine explosion during a patrol. It had affected the nerves in his brain causing him to suffer Parkinson's Disease, occasionally shivering uncontrollably.

At times he was okay though he often needed a wheelchair on hand to steady him but generally he could walk independently when free from an attack.

He was sitting at the party next to Terry and both were busy filling their stomachs with the entire serve-yourself goodies. Lined up on the large dining table, they were actually oblivious of Catherine, Dennis and Adam's issues and were really into the celebration.

Eddy's wife had left him as she could no longer cope with the stress and pressures of looking after a disabled husband who was regularly incontinent of urine and faeces. She had dumped him at the caregivers' home to be looked after.

Eddy was very funny and witty; he often saw the funny side of things and cracked jokes with staff that seemed to be his way of coping with his situation. He would often say to a member of staff, "I am broke; I need to rob a bank."

"In your wheelchair?" staff reminded him.

"Yes! I'll give the police a run for their money. They can't catch me in this chair; I'll fly away; have you forgotten I can make this wheelchair fly?" he ribbed, looking at the team for reaction.

"Someone is having a laugh, "replied Florence, a supporting member of staff who often delighted in looking after Eddy. Eddy was one of the staff's favourites because of his unassuming nature and ability to put smiles on people's faces; making light of his situation.

"Honestly, I can do with some lager and a ciggie to wash down this good meal. Hey, don't look away, Carol Magnum - you are our highly-respected manager. Beer, please!" he repeated, this time louder which made everyone burst into laughter.

Even Carol saw the funny side of the joke and promptly ordered staff to oblige. As soon as he got hold of a can of beer, others followed suit and before long, everyone was drunk and had to be supported to their various rooms to sleep it off. Even Missus was drunk and had to retire early to her stuffed bed.

Everyone had a field day except Dennis and Adam who kept appearing and disappearing; but no one cared what they had been up to.

The next day revealed that loads of Adam's clothes had been torn up. Nothing remained in his wardrobe; even his belts were ripped into bits. Dennis claimed that he did it because Adam did not allow him to dance with Cathy. Adam was furious and staff struggled to calm him down.

There were more staff drafted into the shift to mind Dennis as no-one could predict what next he had up his sleeve. The incident was reported to Carol Magnum who ordered that money be taken out of Dennis' petty cash to pay for the replacement of Adam's ripped clothes.

They acted with great urgency which saved the day as Adam was quickly purchased new clothes. Dennis had to be temporarily moved to a sister care home for a couple of days for his own safety while Adam calmed down.

CHAPTER NINE
HOME VISIT

Dennis Arthur was escorted to his family home for a visit at his father's request because he had a severe cold and could not visit as earlier promised. Frank Priye was down to support him on the visit. It had always been a routine to buy a 'Get well card' for any of his patients' relatives who were not well; in the case of Dennis's father, he would make a special effort to choose the best card.

Dennis loved his father dearly and would occasionally say, "Papa, Papa," in the home each time a parent came visiting their son or daughter. When that happened more regularly, staff took note and subsequently arranged for a family visit for him.

On the way to the nearby ASDA shopping complex located along the motorway, Frank and Dennis had to make the short journey by foot. Dennis was not one to ever let go of any bottle top or small bits and pieces which he always picked up along the way. He kept them to play with because they were very important to him.

With Frank by his side as they strolled to buy the 'get well card,' Dennis suddenly branched off into the motorway to pick up a Coca Cola bottle top to add to his collection. It all happened in a flash and before Frank could intervene, Dennis was already in the middle of the road, bending down to pick it up.

Amid the torrent of traffic, each driver struggled to avoid running him over and at the same time to avoid collision with other cars. Dennis was a huge man and

Frank was virtually helpless to get him out of the traffic. Like a bolt from the blue, a fast car moving at top speed appeared from nowhere and brushed Dennis off the road with its fender and side mirrors; luckily, Frank also pulled him off the motorway.

This all happened at the same time as if pre-planned but he ended up with minor bruises and cuts on his feet and side of his arms, and had to be rushed to the accident and emergency department of St George's Hospital for treatment.

Frank rang the manager, Carol, to report the incident and loads of incident forms were filled out. Dennis's family were not too happy about the incident but were not interested in taking the case any further because they knew how well Frank supported the residents and believed it was probably out of his hands to have stopped it.

Dennis spent a month in the hospital before his discharge but made the lives of his doctors and nurses a Hell on Earth with his aggressive attitude, hitting anyone he perceived to be a stranger or meddling in his affairs. So they came up with the idea of having the constant presence of his familiar care home attendants before any commencement of treatment.

There were no broken bones but medication and plasters were placed on the bruises but as soon as the nurses left, he tore them off his body. The process had to be repeated several times a day to ensure that he didn't end up with infections.

With Dennis out of the way, Adam ruled in the home and no-one could challenge him. Missus was hungrily eating her dinner in a hidden corner of the passageway when suddenly, Adam kicked the bowl from beneath her. Without hesitation, she rushed at him and blessed him with sharp claws which she sank into his fat buttocks. It happened in a flash and she quickly disappeared into the room and under Muriel's bed.

That was not the first time Adam had played silly games with Missus and one of the prime reasons why they never got on. As soon as Muriel saw the speed with which Missus tore into her room, she knew there was a problem. Adam had few deep scratches on his buttocks, but the staff were not aware as he covered it with his underpants.

He was quite self-sufficient and looked after his personal care himself, with very minimal staff support. He dared not report the incident, having been warned several times over by staff and management to leave Missus alone; so he bore his pains quietly and seemed to have kept well away from Missus, at least, for the time being.

The next morning, Missus was at the top of the stairs while Adam was at the foot. Both caught sight of each other and Missus stared directly at him as if to say, "Gotcha bum and don't fuck wiv me! Serves you right" and quickly disappeared once again, not knowing that Adam was equally scared of her. He quickly left through the back door lift to his room and remained indoor all day nursing his bleeding backside. Except for occasionally coming down for a cigarette, he kept well away from Missus whom he saw as a monster for having the guts to attack him.

As Muriel looked out through her window, she could see some flecks of ice floating gently down as they quietly dropped on the playground nearby and everywhere else; it was winter time and she knew she had to wrap up warm; the heating system in the house had broken

down weeks ago with staff and management giving residents one excuse after another.

Muriel reached out to Missus and queried who was chasing her; the poor cat kept mute, having chosen to take the law into her own hands and damn the consequences. She just purred in response to the question and both soon fell asleep.

CHAPTER TEN

YOU DON'T LIKE IT; YOU LUMP IT!

Evelyn Normandy was encouraged to attend some activity lessons in her local school. Initially, she was up for it and really enjoyed the knitting lessons and went along for several weeks until, suddenly, a new student intake was introduced to join her group.

At an instant, she took a dislike to one new student and literally stopped attending college, refusing to tell anyone what her problem was. Every effort to get to the bottom of the matter proved futile; at one point, her key-worker had to work out a college transfer for her to a neighbouring school which she automatically accepted and everything returned to normal.

A couple of months later during a friendly discussion with one of the staff, she mentioned that her late uncle was still alive. When probed further, she opened up that the new student in her former college had looked every inch like him and that was why she could not function there.

She mentioned in passing that another middle-aged man kept ogling her and she didn't know what he wanted. She was encouraged to report problems to the school authorities so they could issue him with a warning.

Evelyn was very good with her hands and voice and she occasionally sang to Dennis when she really wanted to stir things up, and make everyone jealous including Catherine, who appeared to be confused about which of the guys she really fancied as she treated both of them with the same endearment.

One day as Evelyn kept singing, mischievous Catherine went and forcibly pulled the chair from behind her so that she fell on her backside when she tried to sit down after her lovely rendition. Everyone was angry apart from Catherine who felt she had got her own back.

"Hahaha! I might not be able to sing but I can pull chairs!" she said coyly.

A lot of people did not hear what she was saying because of her muffled nasal sounds but Jasmine, her key worker, heard her and promised to report it to the management but she never did because she did not get on well with Evelyn's key worker who never saw anything good in how she did her work and had made that clear to her during the last staff meeting.

They were always on each other's case; even Carol, the manager, didn't feel she had to intervene. "They are both adults and should sort themselves out or bugger off; I've got loads of work to do," she often said with a wicked smile.

At one of the home meetings, James Cardigan, a staff member, raised the issue and pointed out Carol's lack of intervention on the brewing issues between the two staff. He noted that it was unhealthy to have employees bickering with each other.

He was still talking when Carol furiously shouted him down, "Yeah, you all have been talking about me, yeah? I heard that one, but you know what? You don't like it, you lump it!" She pointed her index finger to the floor.

She puffed, "I run this place – I am the manager; so you don't like it? Tough!"

Everyone was afraid to take the issue any further as she appeared to be friendly and powerful with the people at the top.As in most cases when Carol felt cornered, she often came up kicking and scratching with the assertion, "I am the manager!"

That kept everyone quiet and often stopped them from taking complaints any further for fear of reprisal or worse still, losing their jobs.

A new resident, Jack Nikla, was brought into the home. He was a lovely 32-year old gentleman who minded his own business. After they made a general assessment of him and he was found satisfactory, he was given a room next to Dennis; whether both men would get on as friends with mutual respect for each other was to be seen as they kept passing each other in utter silence. Dennis had always been the gentle giant of the home and it surprised everyone that they didn't talk but everyone kept watching.

Jack had spent his fourth week in the house. The girls fancied his athletic build and general skills with a guitar. Catherine was reported to have given him a home-made cupcake; with a smile, she'd muttered, "Be my piece of cake." Jack accepted the cake innocently with a gentleman's, "Thank you!"

Everyone was watching the telly, or pretending to, in the living room. They heard her clearly; some wondered what was going on while others simply ignored it and concentrated on their cigarettes, puffing away.

Rumour had it that Catherine was desperate for a baby; she confided in Agnes Kufour, her support key worker, after they had visited New Town Shopping Centre and seen a woman carrying a newborn baby. Catherine instantly wanted one. Thinking it was for sale, she asked, "Where in here can we buy one? I want a baby girl," she cried to Agnes.

"Babies are not for sale," Agnes replied. Catherine's not-too-severe learning disability often presented her with problems in understanding certain things, especially when she was agitated. That happened to her occasionally but most of the time she was alright if she complied with her daily medication requirements.

"People get pregnant and give birth to babies," explained Agnes.

"How?" Catherine queried and wondered with curiosity.

"I will tell you when we get home," Agnes promised as she tried to get her mind on to something else but knowing Catherine, she would try anything to get what she wanted. She was one of those people with a very strong independent mind; give her an inch, she would take a mile and fight for it when cornered.

Agnes knew a problem was brewing but hoped Catherine would forget all about the woman with the baby girl.

It was a quiet Sunday morning and Adam was back from a church service. His parents were strong Catholics and raised him a Catholic and he never missed the early morning mass. His care plan stated that he should never live anywhere that was not close to a Catholic Church so that he could go there to, "worship his God," as his mother would often unequivocally mention.

She, a very devout Catholic, went to regular mass. "We could not continue to keep him with us as his mental health deteriorated after joining his post code gang and did drugs with them. That turned his head; he got in trouble, killed someone, and went to prison. He's a handful and we couldn't keep him with us. I knew our Lord Jesus and his mother, Virgin Mary, would look after my son," she often narrated to staff each time she visited.

Just back from an early morning mass, broke and with no cigarettes, Adam hoped that Muriel would send him off to buy her some. That would be like hitting a jackpot as his craving for a cigarette was getting a stronger hold on him by the minute.

"Please, can you spare me a cigarette? I'll pay you back on Monday when I get my dole?" he begged Muriel who pretended he wasn't there and was busily puffing and smoking her cigarettes in amused silence.

Adam repeated his appeal and was close enough to wrestle her to the floor over a stick of tobacco when Jack Nikla entered the smoking room by chance, saw Adam's state and said, "Hello mate; want a cigarette? I've got a spare one. You can pay me back next week, alright?" as he threw him a Benson & Hedges.

"Thanks, mate!" he shouted, and quickly grabbed it with both hands before Jack could change his mind. He was so happy to accept the kind gesture. Jack was a life-saver, so Adam thought, as he could have knocked Muriel over and forcibly taken her cigarette. He had been so close to doing that; in fact, he had done so in the past and could still do it again.

Home sanctions or not, he would bear any punishment that came with his often erratic behaviour. He had no qualms about that. As long as he had the cigarette in his hands, nothing else mattered.

Catherine barely entered the smoking lounge as a non-smoker but when she did, she was only there for trouble and to tell someone off; this time it was Muriel.

"You fucking let your fucking cat eat my home-made cup cake…" with both hands on her waist swinging side to side, craning her neck towards Muriel as she homed in on her victim, "…which I kept under my table in my room. Let me tell yah; me fucking want it replaced, okay? Me want me cupcake back and now! This shit keeps happening in here; I've had enough!"

"Good, then! Do yah worst. I didn't eat your fucking cup cake, why come to me?" Muriel replied as if nothing had happened.

"Well, your fucking cat did."

"I am not my fucking cat, am I?" she replied quietly.

Catherine was visibly shaking with rage and was so close to attacking Muriel when Frank overheard her and quickly came in to calm the situation by promising to escort Catherine to the shop to buy a replacement for her; that appeared to do the trick.

Afterwards, the peers were not on talking terms for a while as they kept showing off and winding each other up, stirring jealousy using innuendos, catch-phrases and swear words freely. It was a cold war which staff simply ignored as they knew it wouldn't last. They'd been down that road before; so it was not new.

The same thing that separated the women also brought them together. Missus was a lovely cat and everyone loved her including Catherine. It was only a matter of time before she got in her usual low mood and then she would begin to look for Missus to cuddle and snuggle up to for comfort.

CHAPTER ELEVEN

ADAM'S MOVING ON

Adam looked forward to moving on to his own flat. He had scaled the difficult hurdle of his placement assessment. The future looked good and he couldn't wait to share the good news with anyone who visited. He was seen freely giving out cigarettes to fellow smokers and sweets and chocolates to non-smokers.

Two months later, his placement was yet to be finalised as a suitable flat had not been found. That made him so impatient that he constantly needed staff to encourage and support him psychologically, telling him that the good news was that he had scaled the biggest hurdle and only had to be patient to get suitable accommodation.

After a few weeks, his care-coordinator arrived with good news: suitable accommodation had finally been found for him. Adam was so excited that he started singing reggae; Bob Marley and the Wailers',

"One love...let's get together and feel alright."

Those who knew him well were surprised at him singing. Worse still was his choice of song.

"One love," Muriel teased quietly. "What does Adam know about love for that matter? He is a very selfish and winner-takes-all individual who would not have anything to do with charitable events whatsoever, a Shylock and his pound of flesh," she winked.

Frank Priye was the key-worker who had supported him. New clothes and toiletries purchased and packed, he was ready to go. Everything was packed into the home's van and the driver was ready to drop him off to his new place which was just about five kilometres away.

Adam rushed off to see Catherine. He was seen whispering something in her ear and she was suddenly very attentive to him to everyone's surprise. Even Dennis became so worried that he might lose out that he never said goodbye to Adam when he finally left. Adam had a weird belief that someday, Catherine might move in with him when he settled down in his new one-bedroom flat.

His next step remained to be seen. A couple of weeks later, everyone appeared to have forgotten all about Adam Slater and had generally moved on with their lives. Even Catherine was not bothered, to say the least, while Dennis ruled the roost once again; this time, unchallenged.

The home was full again as a new resident had moved in. His name was Catalogue Kato and he was of Jamaican parentage. He had a little puppy, a retiever, called Angela, who soon had a run-in with Missus; she kept chasing her all over the house, barking and jumping.

At first Missus thought she was playing but she soon realised the puppy was a minor predator who needed to be taught a lesson or two. One wished that Angela knew what Missus was made of. If she did, she would never stray near her - though she was soon to find out.

One Sunday afternoon after the roast dinner, Angela quickly gulped her own dinner and made a beeline for Missus's food. Missus never liked her food piping hot; she was in the habit of waiting for it to cool down before eating. She arrived in time to find Angela licking the plate.

Missus pounced on Angela and almost had her for dinner. But for Frank who intervened on time, it would be Angela's last meal and obituary. The attack was a payback; a combination of all the harassment she had endured at the hands of Angela ever since she had arrived.

"Good on, you; good on, you!" chirped Patience who heard the painful agony Angela suffered in the hands of Missus as she unleashed her brutal attack on her before Frank's rescue. From that moment on, she learned her lessons and stayed away from Missus.

Adam enjoyed his liberty at his new flat and had a carer visit him twice a week to ensure he took his medication and helped him to clean his flat. But Adam's freedom meant that no-one had no control over who Adam chose as his friends.

Occasionally, he visited the local pub for lunch or dinner and a pint of lager. There he met with different kinds of people he made friends with. He was also a very good snooker player and he enjoyed playing with others but he soon learnt that he could play for money and began winning some quick money for himself.

At times he returned home with strangers he called friends and was gradually introduced to things that might not work in his favour. His occasional checks by his appointed professionals became lax as he often put up barriers and invisible walls that made some of his social workers quietly scared of him.

"Move them on and free the beds," said Carol Magnum. "You have to cross the 't's and dot the 'i's if you really want to remain in this job and still be relevant; otherwise, consider yourself dead...that's what the authorities want from you. Paperwork; if it's not written down, it didn't happen, so they believe," she concluded as she chatted to some members of staff at meetings.

Waving a warning finger around, she instructed, "You didn't hear me say that!"

Adam gradually became well-known at the Red Lion Pub as a regular in the evenings and a champion snooker player. That earned him more money and friends; you can't have one without the other.

Johnny Klash, of white British and Jamaican parentage, with lengthy and very unkempt dreadlocks, came to him with a proposition; knowing that he had a criminal past and was a mental health patient still under observation, Adam's situation provided a perfect cover for Johnny's underworld business. Johnny started off by paying regular visits to the Red Lion to meet with Adam and often played snooker with him. Most often he offered to play for a lot of money which he often let Adam win - either by chance or design.

Out of five games, he might pretend to have struggled too hard to win one of the five turns played and that meant big money for Adam. Before he knew it, they had become inseparable friends; then Johnny gradually introduced him back into drugs, using him as his drug courier with minimal commission for any successful sale.

Adam slipped into his old life of crime. He soon turned his new flat into a drug den where customers came to relax and do drugs. The locals soon began noticing different faces coming and going even in the middle of the night. There were occasional fights between unfriendly customers, or some who simply refused to pay.

Adam knew that if those guys didn't pay, he had to make the payment; most often, it was deducted from his commission which he never liked. More often than not, he fought them to get his money back. Already, he owed over £500 in cocaine he had used for himself and was struggling to pay his dealer back. His dealer was so happy

Adam owed money as that kept him indebted and obedient and made him serve his master well without questions.

Johnny Klash was a ruthless drug dealer who drove a very expensive open-roof coupe BMW car, the latest series, and always carried a short loaded revolver concealed in the large pocket of his jacket for protection and as a means of threat to his debtors.

In disagreements, he rubbed his large fingers on it as a matter of first warning to behave and hand over his money before things got really bad. Once or twice he had pistol-whipped Adam who then lashed out and fought him like a wounded lion; he was high on heroin and was not able to balance Johnny's books for the week.

"You should fucking give me £2,500 for two weeks gone. How come you're just giving me this shit, £1550; where's my balance before wring yah bloody neck?" Johnny yelled.

He had built his entire life on drug money and tough reputation. Already high on drugs, Adam shouted, "Will you fucking leave me flat now before me kill somebody? You pig, yah tot yah've got a slave to boss around yeah!?" he queried with a rush of adrenalin.

Without warning, a scuffle ensued and Johnny pistol-whipped Adam on his forehead causing it to swell. Adam blindly charged at him like a bull and landed several head-butts on his face, smashing blood, teeth, and guts. Johnny slumped, his legs buckled under him and with a mighty thud he landed heavily on the dirty carpet and blacked out.

His pistol fell from his hands and Adam picked it up. He shot him at close range; narrowly missed his forehead by inches but the bullet burnt through his left ear leaving Johnny with less than half of his ears.

Adam's wild anger made his whole body shake, especially the hand holding the trigger. He shot at him again but heard only a click; no more bullets. Then he threw the gun in the bin, dragged Johnny out of his flat and left him lying beside his car, bleeding on the cold floor of the parking lot.

He opened his driver's door wide, spat and kicked at Johnny's body and shouted, "Fucking idiot, now get into yah car and disappear. Next time am gonna cremate yah, yah won't live to say hello to anyone no more; got dat?"

He slightly lifted him by his shoulders, bent his back over and gave him a very good kick on the bum and that jolted Johnny as he jumped to his feet and fell inside his car. He fumbled for his car keys which were still in his pocket, started the engine and drove off like a lunatic without the headlights on, bleeding all the way as Adam returned to his flat to nurse his injuries.

CHAPTER TWELVE

LET IT RING; WE DON'T PICK UP IF IT'S THEM!

Mariam, a seventeen-year old girl and a student, returned home to her mom with mental health problems. It all started one day when people in her neighbourhood who knew her as a child saw her behaving strangely in her school uniform and rang her mom.

Her father was a British sailor who was always on a ship somewhere, spending six months at a time on the high seas. As a result, Sarai, her mom, was the only one left to look after Mariam and her younger brother, Philips.

When Mariam's mother got the news of her daughter's behaviour, it was almost too late as she was already in coma after being knocked down by a careless hit-and-run driver. Eye witness accounts had it that she deliberately kept running towards approaching vehicles and was unlucky to run into one that couldn't slow down to stop and avoid her.

A passerby called an ambulance which arrived at the scene to move her to the nearest hospital where Sarai found her on a life-support machine.

No-one believed she would make it but months later, she started showing visible signs of recovery. Her cognitive system appeared to be slightly impaired but occasionally she could remember things in her past. She could even recall how her life turned that negative corner but with a wobbly gait and a short memory span.

One day, Mariam told how she was bullied in school by some of her mates and was forced to try a joint of marijuana and some lines of cocaine. She had constantly refused to take them several times in the past despite their bullying tactics; but her mates changed their attitude towards her. They alienated her and became very nasty towards her. They would not invite her out for a drink and to parties. They told her the bullying would stop if she joined in their smoking and drug habits.

To make matters worse, they would return to school and talk about how much fun they had at parties and their exploits and conquests. As a young woman trying to find her way in life, she wanted to have fun and party experiences but not with drugs.

Mariam kept to the straight and narrow path until one fateful day after school, she was invited by her group of friends to the school's back garden where they forced her to smoke, spliff, and ingest cocaine; five of them forcefully held her to the ground and throttled her by the neck almost to the point of unconsciousness until she had no choice but to do their bidding. As soon as they finished with her, they disappeared.

Hours later, she managed to scramble to her feet and had no clue where she was or where she was going but found herself on the motorway as she later learnt. She was told how she kept chasing after any vehicle that turned up until her luck ran out when she was knocked over.

Sarai was stuck with Mariam who became increasingly dependent. Her mom had to leave her well-paid job to cater for her while they all lived on her father's income. On one bright Sunday morning, it all came to a head when Mariam sneaked out of her bedroom to the family swimming pool behind the house. She used to be a very good swimmer but her illness had taken a toll on her ability. She dived into the pool and almost drowned, letting out a very loud shout as she realised she was sinking.

Her mom, who was then at the back of the kitchen doing the laundry, was quick to run to her rescue but not without Mariam having gulped a belly-full of water. The pool water mixed with chlorine meant she had to be taken to the hospital for treatment. As time for her discharge drew closer, Sarai had had enough and she called up the social services to find a suitable residential home for Mariam as it dawned on her that she needed lots of additional help to support her daughter.

She was then moved to High Street Care Homes where Dennis, Adam, Catherine, Jack, Muriel and others lived. It was like a community of care homes for people with diverse disabilities ranging from mental health issues, elderly care, needs and young offenders to learning disabilities, among others.

Adam and Dennis were quick to visit Mariam separately to introduce themselves - probably as the major power brokers of the home. However, they were quick to run each other down in front of her; Adam referred to Dennis as the, "stupid boy who was always a copycat." He continued, "You see, I am the big boss around here! You know what; don't let that stupid Dennis lie to you. If anyone messes with you, just call me; I'll sort 'em out, okay?"

Dennis was his usual smiley self, introduced himself and showed a bit of his arm muscle and said, "Any problem…call me?" and soon left to her bewilderment.

She seemed to like the bad boys whom she referred to as, "two self-obsessed individuals" when her mother asked how she was coping in her new home. She told her about the bad boys and they laughed them off as mere attention-seeking young men.

With more time on her hands, Sarai went back to work as a legal secretary at Jon Bons & Sons Solicitors. She could mostly call the home by phone or in person at weekends. She soon appeared to be aright pain in the ass with some care staff and nurses at the home as she often grilled the staff with a barrage of questions; some very personal and unrelated to her daughter.

At one point a member of staff was sacked because of an unfounded allegation from her. As time went by, they had had enough of her so they ignored her calls. It was so cleverly done that whenever she turned up in person, she would see a lot of broad smiling faces.

They would usually say almost as though they were singing in a chorus: "Madam Sarai, would you like to play backgammon with your daughter? She appears to love the game so much. Ever since she beat Mellisa at the game, she thinks she can take on the world!"

Sarai would respond rather nonchalantly, "No, thanks for the offer; let's save that for another day when I visit again but right now, I'd like to spend time with my daughter."

"What did you have for dinner?" queried Sarai.

"Oh mom, it was mashed potatoes, sausages, veggies and gravy."

"Oh dear! Was this not what you had when I was here three days ago?"

"Mom, please don't start! We are used to it," Mariam replied, expecting her mom to change the topic.

"If this is the case, I need to see your manager at once to change the cook. The menu needs to be changed. What happened to healthy foods like salmon and vegetables? No wonder you lot look like cows and pigs for slaughter. How much do you weigh now since you moved in here?" she attacked.

"Mom, just don't go there; I've only been here for two weeks. Don't let them move me again the way you let them move me from Grail Hillcroome. If that happens again, I'll make sure they never let you anywhere near me again; understood?" Mariam warned.

Ignoring her daughter, Sarai asked if she could have a cup of tea; her way of masking her daughter's threat.

"Ah, what a nice cup of tea! Your dad is away again; now to Australia. He promised to be back in time for Christmas. Do you miss him?" she asked.

"Of course I do. Dad doesn't bother me the way you do; he understands how I feel. I wish you could be like that," she added.

"I am now the monster then; when all I do is to look after my own daughter," she began rubbing her eyes in pretence as though crying; Mariam simply ignored her and quickly changed the topic to which presents she would like for Christmas.

CHAPTER THIRTEEN

WAKE ME UP AT 10

Catherine was due for an appointment for a smear test at her doctor's surgery. She felt so scared that she made it everybody's business.

"You know; it's due tomorrow," she said.

"What are you talking about?" muttered Muriel, with smoke oozing from her mouth and nostrils.

"My cervical smear test, of course; don't tell me you haven't got a clue about it," she worried.

"Oh what the fuck! Ladies go through this every now and again, and why do you think you can make my life hell cos yah want to go for the fucking check-up? Will you just go away and let me enjoy my fag? Who fucking cares whether you go or not, and who fucking cares whether you tested positive or negative? You do your business; I do mine and once again stop stressing everyone out in here cos you wanna go for some fucking smear test!" Muriel blurted as she shifted her bulky body, and rudely excused herself.

"Will you give me a shout at ten then? That's my appointment time," Catherine interjected.

"Just fuck off!" thundered Muriel who was at the edge of her rocking chair in the T.V lounge. She was seething with anger and wished Catherine would dare to inch closer so she could grab her clothes, pull her closer, and teach her some good lessons.

Luckily, Catherine was few metres beyond her reach. She soon got the message and disappeared to her room. Poor Missus tried to follow her but Catherine was too upset. She banged her door so loudly that the whole staff rushed upstairs, in a fluster, thinking someone had been badly hurt in an accident only to find out that Catherine was just in her usual way expressing her anger.

CHAPTER FOURTEEN

THE RETURN OF JOHNNY KLASH

Adam staggered home with so many drugs and so much confusion in his system; he fell on his dirty rug and fell fast asleep. He woke up the next morning with a terrible pain and hunger for food. He looked around and could barely recognise his flat as everything looked terribly untidy and unkempt. He dragged himself up and held on to his sofa for support.

He could see what appeared to be a wad of money lying a few feet away from him; he edged closer for a better look and found that it was money; he wondered how it got there. He also saw one shoe of a pair of trainers and wondered whose it was. He looked every corner of his flat for the second shoe but could not find it. The trainer appeared familiar because he had seen someone wear it many times.

After a moment's thought, he recalled what had happened the night before. It all made sense and he could remember that the cash was the £1,550 drug money he had earlier on given to Johnny Klash. He also remembered that he had had a big fight with the drugs bully and a few bullets were fired; was the man dead or still alive?

He panicked as he thought about it. If Johnny was dead, it would be good news. He would only have the police and the court to contend with but if he was still alive, "it would be jungle justice all the way. I am a dead man walking," he told himself.

He quickly got up and rushed to the bin out on the side street. He looked inside and could see the shot gun he had thrown in there as a silly method of disposal. "I'm prepared for the worst in my crazy world; one minute you are in a psychiatric hospital or a home and the next you are in hand-cuffs cooling off in a police cell or even back in prison," he ruminated.

Adam quickly dipped his hands in the bin. With a dirty hand towel, he gently picked up the shot gun and put it straight into his trouser pocket. Looking around furtively and satisfied that no-one else was watching, he gently sneaked back into his flat and was soon engulfed in his thoughts.

Having someone like Johnny Klash on your back was everyone's nightmare; even the bravest would cower. Adam dreaded that thought and would be happy to have that cup pass him by.

He knew he had to move home immediately and lie very low; no more snooker and visiting the pub for a pint. That was a big task but he was ready to brave that by changing his pub. He had some money to play with but had to be very careful.

The next day, Adam paid a quick visit to St Helier's Hospital in Surrey. Almost everyone there knew him and appeared to get on well with him.

He went straight to the receptionist, "Hi Karen, you alright mate? I am wondering if you saw a bloke here last night with smelly dreadlocks and gold-capped teeth - he's a mate of mine. He probably was here around 11pm last night. Did you see a bloke like that?"

"How tall was your mate?"

"He should be about six feet," replied Adam.

"Does he drive a classy, silver BMW car with a new registration number?"

"I think so but I'm not fussy about cars; I prefer buses and bikes; eco-friendly, you know?" Adam murmured.

"Yes, I think he was here yesterday. He was battered by some bloke, he told us; someone owed him some money and other stuff. We could barely make out a word of what he was saying before he passed out. He bled badly," Karen confirmed.

"Thank you," Adam hurried out of the St Helier's emergency reception unit. "So he survived it," he wondered. "I'd better disappear from my house for a while. Johnny doesn't take defeat lying down. I know he's gonna bump me off next time he sees me; it's either him or me next time around. I now have to sleep with one eye open. I've got his money and some of his crack cocaine; he has used me for so long to peddle his drugs, exploiting my psychiatric illness.

"Not anymore!" he continued. "Now he won't let me owe him; worse still, he pays ridiculous commissions. He's daft enough to believe I should be risking it all for such a pittance; fuck him!" he raged. "I know he won't let that go, never!" he admitted.

Adam chose to sleep rough thenceforth until his problems with Johnny were sorted out. Now he would have to fight the gang of rough sleepers as well. Adam was very street-wise and that marked him out as different from Dennis Arthur who had lived a sheltered life most of the time before being moved into care. He quickly got a new sleeping bag for himself, confided in some of his street gang members and charged them to always have his back and help him watch out for Johnny Klash.

He had some money and crack and could be very generous with his mates. With money and crack cocaine, he could buy his gang members' loyalty and respect. He became a Don among them. They practically worshipped him as he constantly blew all he had on them.

Despite resorting to rough sleeping, he never gave up his flat and would always send some gang members to do a bit of surveillance work for him before he returned home briefly to pick a thing or two but never to pass the night.

He also visited his former home to say hello to staff and residents and most importantly to see Catherine and figure out what

Dennis was up to. He bought some cheap, contraband cigarettes on a BOGOF deal (buy one, get one free) as gifts for some - particularly Alan, whom he regarded as a friend.

Catherine was a non-smoker and he got her some cakes, flowers, and packets of sweets. To Adam, she was just his girlfriend and he didn't bother about what Dennis did in his absence. As funny as that sounded, Dennis did nothing and barely spoke to Catherine when Adam was absent; they both passed each other quietly on the corridor without even a 'hello'; one wondered what the trigger was as soon as Adam arrived.

Dennis would get closer and friendlier with Catherine to scare off Adam. That hardly worked as Adam appeared to be a tough nut to crack. Adam rapped at the door and was let in by a staff member, "Oh

Adam! How are you? You've remembered to visit us today. You're welcome; please come in and have a seat."

"Thanks, Josephine," he replied, with a broad smile on his face. Dennis saw him and smiled, walked past him and went to sit close to Catherine as Adam shared his presents with those he liked. Adam gave Dennis a stern look - enough to warn him off Catherine. Whether it worked remained to be seen as Dennis continued to stand his ground without flinching; both men knew how mad the other was and tried as much as possible to stay away.

Oblivious, Catherine still mourned having no baby to play with. She wanted a real baby and kept believing she would one day be able to convince Josephine to buy her one from Sainsbury's.

CHAPTER FIFTEEN

THEY ARE NOT YOUR FRIENDS

Dawn broke with the early morning wind blowing ceaselessly. The trees and flowers danced to its rhythm. It was Christmas morning!

Staff on duty were up for a windfall of double pay for working on such a special day. Patience, the African parrot, was still in her metal cage chirping and calling names of everyone she could remember. She also kept saying, "It's Christmas; it's Christmas; it's Christmas," non-stop.

Apparently, Madam Loveline had told her the night before that the next day was Christmas. She knew it was a very special day in England; there was no public transport and everyone stayed at home with their families and loved ones. It was the time visitors to the home would always come to her for a chat; she could make more friends or enemies depending on how they treated her. She also knew that some bullies like Dennis would be home with their families and wouldn't come over to taunt her or steal her nuts.

Everyone appeared to have woken up earlier than usual. Muriel and Madame Loveline loved to attend the local Catholic Church for the morning mass and Christmas was the only day they attended church.

"To prepare myself and wash clean before my Lord Jesus Christ; to usher in the New Year's blessings," professed Muriel, who appeared to be more spiritual than the others in the home.

Frank Priye was also on shift as he too loved to be on duty on Christmas Day. Carol Magnum, the home manager, was unofficially on duty as well; she chose to spend a half-day interacting with her staff and residents. Her presence seemed like a spoiler's portion for everyone who wished she had rather stayed at home with her family.

"She's here and everyone walks on egg shells; no mistakes; constantly looking over your shoulder and the occasional telling off when things don't go her way. I would have cancelled my shift had I known she would be here today," regretted Josephine.

The Christmas dinner was the best and appeared to taste a lot better in the home; not that it was different from the usual meal but the serene atmosphere of Christmas was the icing on the cake. Everyone dressed and behaved their best and sat down to watch the Christmas carols being sang by choirs on the telly, with occasional treats passed around to sweeten the day.

Appearing worried, Catherine came down with her dressing not up to scratch as a lady. Josephine was on hand to find out what the matter was. She offered emotional and psychological support, sitting side by side with her. Carol Magnum walked past the first time and saw them chatting. The next time she walked past, Josephine was helping Catherine knot her shoelace.

"You don't have to do that; she's not your friend or family. Let her do it by herself," she snapped and stormed away without waiting for an answer or finding out what had transpired.

Josephine wished the earth would open up to swallow her; she was so cross at her manager's reaction and off-hand behaviour and promised herself to bring it up in her next supervision meeting.

Missus was at the back of the home, hopping up to snatch some leftovers hanging out at the bottom of Patience's metal cage. "Stop that; stop that," chirped Patience, as she found it ridiculous. They were both good friends and Missus could have asked and she would have no qualms about sharing her food.

A lot of visitors had been to the house to see their loved ones for the season and everyone was amazed at Patience's intelligence and repertoire. She never seemed to ever forget anything she heard just once. Finally, Missus succeeded in getting the piece of bacon hanging loose at the bottom of the cage. She sat quietly in the shadows to enjoy it.

The Christmas party was quite enjoyable; everyone had enough to eat and drink except for Adam who kept swapping seats and looking out the window as if expecting a surprise but he was not the type to share his pain or joy with anyone. He kept everything to himself but staff suspected trouble; others thought there was no need for such suspicion as Dennis was absent.

No one suspected that Adam wore a shot gun everywhere he went; it was nicely hidden in the large pocket of his over-sized trousers with a rugged, over-sized blue, long-sleeve shirt that acted like a perfect cover for the hidden gun which he occasionally fingered to reassure himself.

CHAPTER SIXTEEN

THE MEASURE YOU GIVE

Bala Abubakir became one of the newly-recruited staff at the High Street Care Home after so many left as a result of poor wages and general lack of adequate personnel and material support for the workforce.

He was a charming Caucasian-Jamaican young man in his twenties with amiable looks and very clever, too. You could never catch him out on anything because he would always give a good excuse for his actions or inactions; if you cornered him, you could lose your job because he appeared to be loved by the bosses. He had a way of making people believe in what he said to them; they hardly won an argument.

"These people pay peanuts and they want you to kill yourself doing their dirty work and they receiving the fat pay-check. You know what; the measure they pay, the measure you work. Don't let anyone bloody rip your ass off. Bosses live like kings; we're the scroungers that do all the hard work. No one can justify that; I mean, it is an injustice,"

Bala would often tell his close confidants, pointing his fingers at them, he blasted, "You could drop dead doing this job and the next day, they would bring in the agency to cover your role. No-one will bloody mourn your demise, believe me; and you know what?" he warned. "You never heard me say this. You breathe a word of this to anyone around here, I'll deny I said anything," he concluded, sticking his index finger into the sky; his quiet way of swearing them to secrecy.

For Bala, the workplace was an important platform for socialising rather than working his butt off. He believed in eye-service and as soon as Carol Magnum came to the floor, she would see Bala emptying all bins from room to room, office to office and toilet to toilet non-stop and woe betide anyone who later complained to Carol regarding Bala's laziness. The last person that reported him got a summary dismissal straight away and that appeared to keep others in check.

Bala had warmed his way into the hearts and minds of all the service users and even Missus and Patience as he occasionally fed them with their favourite food he bought with his own money. He took everyone out to the gym and showed them some of his antics. That won everyone over and soon he seemed addicted to the gym. "Working out is the best therapy," he often said.

CHAPTER SEVENTEEN

JOHNNY KLASH IN THE BAHAMAS

Johnny Klash quietly left for the Bahamas Hospital, the birthplace of his parents before they moved over to live in Britain. He wanted to get access to good medical treatment without the nosiness of the British law enforcement authorities.

He would not stand anyone questioning him about his blown off left ear among other injuries. His parents knew his business but could not stop him because the last time they had, he'd beaten them to a pulp and locked them up in the family pantry for two days without food or water.

That taught them to mind their business and leave everything else to fate.

His father was beyond caring while his mother would often visit her local church to pray for his lost son's repentance. Johnny was discharged from the Bahamas Hospital and went straight home to his parents' for full recovery. He used to have a wife before but when she found out what he did for a living, she divorced him. He woke up one day to find a handwritten piece of paper telling him she was sorry to have left him and hoped he would love again.

She never actually told him why she was leaving him; a rough count put the figure at six - the number of women who had done the same thing to him. He was the sort of man who beat up his wife over minor issues like talking to another man on the street or not staying at home waiting for him to return from wherever he had been.

He never discussed his business with anyone and as soon as his parents set their eyes on him, they knew straight away there was a problem, probably police-related. He was their only son and they lived in fear of him as his violent mood swings had no limits. He once bought them a brand new, 50-inch, colour T.V and soon after, they were engaged in an argument. In a flash, he lifted the giant telly off its stand and like a thunder, smashed it against the wall.

Adam Slater was getting closer to Catherine and she was beginning to acknowledge his presence. "Maybe absence makes the heart grow fonder," she thought but kept wondering what the hell was bulging in his pockets.

"I will take you to my new flat," he promised her, "and I will give you a cup of tea and some slices of cake," he added, smiling.

Catherine merely nodded in reply and they both giggled. The little gifts of roses Adam had been giving her seemed to be doing the trick.

"I will visit your flat and play backgammon or snakes and ladders with you." As she looked into his eyes, you could tell it was a different look but you couldn't be too sure with Catherine; her moods swung like a pendulum ball on a piece of thread. To the staff, Adam and Catherine were just ordinary friends and nothing more.

Adam was busily covering his tracks and making sure that he never bumped into Johnny Klash as he knew that might be his end. Johnny had occasionally hung out in his neighbourhood, patiently hoping to spot Adam but to no avail; he was not a man who ever gave up. He lived on the edge and with no conscience.

As Adam shuttled from homelessness to homelessness, he barely retired to his home and only popped in in the middle of the night with his own street gang whose respect he had earned by supporting them to fend off attacks in the past.

One fateful day in April, 2007, Adam was out with his gang at a casino for some games. It was not a good day for them as they lost a lot of money gambling. They left very unhappy and strutted to the nearest bus station to catch the late night bus home.

After barely ten minutes of waiting, a gang member spotted the fellow who dealt them a heavy hand at the casino; in a split second, they pounced on him, mugged and robbed him of his winnings. When they thought he was half-dead, they fled the scene with their loot.

The incident happened not so far away from Catherine's home; so Adam decided to pay her a night visit and damn the consequences. It was 2 am and most of the night staff and residents must have been fast asleep. Having lived there for six years, he knew his way around the home; he thus knew the back gate was rarely locked.

With a push, the gate opened. Drenched from head to toe, he hoped Catherine would welcome him without raising the alarm which would attract unnecessary attention. He walked through the alley and straight to Catherine's door. He knocked softly to be sure he wasn't alerting any concerned ears.

With trepidation, Catherine woke up and moved towards the door.

"Who's there?"she asked softly amidst yawning.

"It's me, Adam. Please open the door for me," he whispered.

She quickly opened the door. "Adam, why are you here?" she asked. "You're soaking wet!"

Adam walked into the room, dripping little pools of rainwater onto the carpet. He grinned sheepishly and moved as if to embrace her. Catherine took a hurried step backwards with a worried look upon her face.

"A bit of rain," he pulled a face. "I came to see my favourite girl and hoped for a kiss and a snuggle, maybe," he winked.

Catherine considered this for a moment. "Well...perhaps, if you take off your wet clothes, we could cuddle under the blankets," she ventured.

Adam didn't need asking twice. He quickly divested himself of his shirt and stepped out of his jeans and pants. He stood there for a moment, stark naked, grinning at Catherine, his eyes full of lust.

Catherine stood rooted to the spot. She had never seen a naked man before; at least not in real life, and certainly not in her bedroom. Her eyes swept over his body and glanced at his manhood fully erect. She blushed with embarrassment and cast her eyes downwards. The first stirrings of fear and uncertainty bubbled up from within her.

Adam, noting her apparent discomfort, laughed at her embarrassment, took her by her hand and led her to the bed. Before she could utter a protest, he lifted the crumpled bed clothes, pushed her onto the bed, and then leapt in beside her, shivering with cold and unspent passion.

He pulled Catherine towards him, then somewhat uncharacteristically, kissed her gently on the lips. She gave the smallest moan which only served to increase his ardour.

"Hey! I'm lying here without a stitch on; it would only be fair if you do same," he said teasingly.

He deftly pulled her night dress up over her quivering body with such determination and purpose that Catherine meekly complied; lifting her arms above her head to facilitate its removal.

"That's better," he whispered.

He kissed her again and finding her lips tightly pursed, he forced them apart with his tongue before plunging it into her opened mouth. Catherine tried to recoil but Adam wasn't going to stop. Adam knew how to get what he wanted. His hands went straight to her breasts; plump, firm, and pretty. He squeezed them roughly, making her wince.

He lifted his head to look at her and saw the fear in her face. "Don't be afraid, my best girl," he whispered. "We are made for each other."

He then moved quickly to cover her body with his, unable to deny himself the pleasure he had come for. He pushed her legs apart with his knees, found her entrance with his probing penis and then plunged into her without further hesitation.

A few thrusts later and Adam was spent. He groaned loudly, rolled off her body and promptly fell asleep with a subtle smile on his face. Catherine lay wide awake. The sharp stab of pain she had experienced when he first thrust into her had subsided. She acknowledged the

raw, stinging throb, and the warm sticky liquid trickling between her legs; she touched and looked and it was a trickle of blood.

She turned her head to look at Adam who was snoring in total oblivion. She laid awake for some time with her mind in a whirl of emotions. One thought stayed with her as she drifted off to sleep, "That was my first time; the ice has been broken. I am no longer a virgin..."

CHAPTER EIGHTEEN

FRANK PRIYE'S TURMOIL

The August rain dropped onto the rooftops like a hail of pellets in the middle of a wet night, serenaded with the ever-present snakey flashes of lightening and a loud, thunderous, resounding sound that sent every creature into a quaky standby mode, all dashing for cover as no-one was in doubt about the mayhem it could cause.

Frank Priye was jolted from his sleep as the unexpected mighty thunder rang out in its compelling, voracious boisterousness that could send even the lion-hearted scampering for safety. It was accompanied by a majestic multitude of lightening forks, striking in different, snaky directions.

Frank safely tucked himself into his duvet but, honestly, he would have preferred hiding under his bed for safety. He pulled his duvet tighter and closer to himself as his only weapon of hope; most people where the same when faced with the force of nature. Nature was always supreme in the face of Mankind who dared not contend with it.

Frank let out a cough and with a quick glance at his Seiko wrist watch; he realised it was 10:30am.

"I have been asleep for the past ten hours; this can't be right," he thought.

He jumped out of his bed half-naked, ran into the bathroom, had a wee, brushed his teeth and had a good shower; it was 11:30am. He grabbed a bowl of porridge with clusters of blueberries and a cup of tea for breakfast. With nothing else to do, he went to his sitting room, turned on the T.V. and tuned in to the BBC News. It always made his day as he was able to switch off worrying and self-pity and focus on the wider news about what was going on outside of himself.

Just as he was beginning to drift away to sleep again, his mobile phone rang. He usually wouldn't answer any anonymous calls at that time because he preferred to know who was calling and he wasn't actually expecting anyone to contact him at that time of the day.

If there was a call, he could see the caller's number; all his friends would be busy at work and he only had few of them. He thought, perhaps, the call might be from some desperate telemarketers who would do anything to sell you products you didn't actually need. Some products could even be dodgy; another reason he wouldn't answer the calls.

"Let them keep ringing, they will soon hang up when no-one answers," he reasoned.

A few minutes later, his mobile phone rang again; this time, the number showed. He picked it up in anger to switch it off but for some reason he looked at it once again. The number was unmistakable; it was from the head office.

"These idiots again," he muttered as he picked up the receiver and gently placed it by his ears. "Hello," he whispered. "Who am I speaking to?" he queried.

"Can I speak to Frank?" the voice rang out. "Yes, Frank speaking," he answered.

"Is that Frank?" the caller repeated. "I am Karen Mackintosh, human resources manager. We need to see you at the head office as soon as possible. A new piece of evidence has turned up; could you please confirm if it would be possible for you to be here tomorrow, 14:00hrs on the dot? It's very important. Can you make it? she snapped.

"Okay, I will. Thanks," Frank agreed and the phone went dead. A new brand of stress and panic hit him; he was going up and down the stairs in his home, confused almost to the point of hysteria.

"The unexpected has happened; what else have they pinned on me this time around? What new evidence?" he worried. "Where do I go from here?" he wondered.

He was soon on the phone to Edward, his best mate. "Hello Edward," he called out. "I am in big trouble!"

"Please calm down, Frank," Edward pleaded. "Are you free tomorrow?"

"They want me at the head office at 2pm tomorrow. I need you to come with me, please," he begged.

"Don't worry. Wait a minute and let me check in my diary." There were a few moments of silence as Edward trawled through the book.

He checked the date and it was all booked up. "I have two pieces of news for you, Frank; one is bad and the other good; which one do you want first?" he boasted.

"Look, this is not something to joke about," Frank shouted. "My head is on the guillotine here and I might never be able to work again if it all goes wrong; just tell me yes or no. I've got no time to gamble on anything now. As you can see I am finished already," he relented.

"Okay! Now listen: the bad news is that my diary is full tomorrow and the good news is that I could ask my boss for a day off so I can be

there to support you; and I don't want you to break down or lose sleep over this because it will all soon be over," Edward added.

"Oh thanks; I am very grateful. I owe you one!" Frank concluded.

CHAPTER NINETEEN
CLINTON, HOME BOY

It was a cold winter morning and Johnny Klash realised he was running out of money. He had half a dozen of his drug pimps dotted around owing him money for drug sales from Adam Slater and Clinton Abbey, a new chap in the care home.

Clinton lost his parents when he was three and had been adopted by a loving couple. He'd had a normal childhood until he gained admission into the University of Cardoso in Edinburgh to study computer engineering; that was his first time leaving home and moving away from the love and care of Mr and Mrs Joel Atkins, his foster parents.

In his first year, he got to know a fellow student who lived in the same hostel apartment. He'd introduced Clinton to cannabis and later, cocaine. His brain could not deal with it - he got addicted and nearly burned the hostel down. He was arrested and charged with arson and spent years in Springfield Psychiatric Hospital. He was later discharged to a lower psychiatric support unit where he got recruited by Johnny Klash.

His foster parents would still come around to visit but wouldn't have him back in their home as they didn't want him to influence their biological children who were young and impressionable

Clinton had problems trusting anyone; he ended up with a hatred for school but loved money and occasional used cocaine. He had no major disability but appeared hyperactive; so he had medication to calm him down. The side effects, however, left him with the telltale signs of a slight mental disorder.

He occasionally used his situation to play the system and blamed it on his mental health when cornered. He often wanted attention and had a way of getting everyone worried and running around to his rescue when he feigned epilepsy.

Over the years, he had perfected these tricks. He also feigned asthmatic attacks though at times these could be real. Staff did not take anything for granted; they always supported him on all occasions.

Six months earlier, before Christmas, Johnny Klash met him at the Red Lion with a couple of guys who appeared to have met each other before. One could tell that they were all there for just one reason; to play snooker for money or bet on horses or football matches.

It was a lucky day as it appeared there were lots of winnings for most players and gamblers and a lot of free beers available as happy winners splashed out on free booze for anyone; just anyone they wanted to make happy.

Johnny Klash appeared on the scene, bought free drinks for the young, impressionable lads whom he wanted to recruit into his plans. That was how he met Clinton Abbey for the very first time. He had a word with him afterwards and recruited him; that was how he got him to deal for him with little or no commission.

Everything went well for a couple of months until Clinton realised what a fool he had been.

"This guy drives a flashy car around to collect his sales only for me to be given a paltry sum. I've been a mug!" he thought.

He began using the drugs and some of the money realised in sales. After a while, he was unable to balance the books for Johnny Klash. Because he couldn't deliver the profits, he became the hunted while Johnny was the hunter; a deadly one at that. He could not bring himself to tell anyone.

He was scared each time he saw a car that looked like Johnny's and soon became very reclusive, refusing to leave home even for a walk or to go shopping. He often came up with excuses to avoid anything outdoors and it became so serious that doctors' appointments were converted to home visits only.

He found a good excuse to avoid going to school and anything that would cause him to leave home. Everyone appeared worried for him and thought it was a new dimension to his illness but some had their reservations. However, no-one wanted to be accused of forcing the residents to do things they didn't want to. Staff did everything to avoid disciplinary actions that could impact on their records so Clinton was left to his own devices.

The situation went on for a couple of months and Johnny Klash was drowning in debts as some other kids, who seemed to have fallen into his drug trap like Clinton Abbey and Adam Slater, owed him money, too. Some of these kids who appeared more brazen ended up with their corpses lying in the streets and alleyways as they got bumped off by Johnny's hit men. The police's inquests turned out to be pointless as no-one was ever arrested or charged with murder.

"You can't con me out of my money and goods and not end your journey six-feet below the earth," Johnny often warned his young recruits on initiation. "That way, you can rest assured that your debts are paid off in full. The dead stay dumb."

The recent number of kids lying in the streets dead, fast became a serious cause for concern to the police and the public alike. As what Johnny was owed increased, so did the dead bodies. He was seriously in debt himself to his major Colombian supplier and resorted to fending him off by paying him out of his own money. The situation was getting critical and he had to do something fast; a minor slip might cost him his life, he reasoned.

Maxwell Skullcracker was a major Colombian drug baron of the underworld. He was a man of little conscience and few words; a brutal nut-case who never suffered fools gladly. He was totally allergic to the use of the words, 'pardon,' or, 'forgive.' Those words were alien to him. There was no such thing as 'second chances.'

He was reported to have once used a chainsaw to destroy his wife for cheating on him, gathering her remains into a bin and setting it on fire; he fed the flames till it all burnt into ashes. His wife's lover watched and waited for his turn. Maxwell ordered his men to hang him on a stake with a cord fastened to his penis and balls and that was all that held his suspended body in mid-air till he died in agony.

He later gave Natasa, their five-year old, only daughter, up for adoption. No one in their right mind would adopt her; so the authorities had to change her name first before any adoption took place. He never looked for her and always said, "She reminded me of her mother."

The mention of Maxwell Skullcracker sent shivers down men's spines, especially his rivals, because they knew he would not spare a thought for anyone who stood in his way. His real name was Maxwell Sparrows but due to to his horrible reputation, his gang mates gave him the alias, 'Skullcracker.' They had lost count of the number of people who had simply disappeared for either disobeying his instructions or non-payment of what they owed him.

He had never known his father and his mother was a Colombian local prostitute. When she realised that she had gotten pregnant, she sought termination. She chose to do it herself using a local herbal concoction noted for the termination of pregnancy. She nearly bled to death but the pregnancy was still intact. She was then advised to keep it as further attempts to end it could cost her, her life.

That was it, she thought, the baby had to go up for adoption. She wouldn't bring up a child she wasn't ready for; the shame would definitely tear her family apart as they thought she had a high-powered job in the city of Bogota, Columbia, as her entire extended family lived off her prostitution without any knowledge of it.

At the time, she was engaged to be married to Pius Krono in her native village fifty miles away from the city of Bogota and the last thing on her mind was to let him down. She just needed to earn enough money to quit the trade, but with a pregnancy, she didn't know what to do. As time went by, she decided to cut ties with all her family members including Pius Kronos, her fiancé.

Thinking again, she really wanted to experience motherhood. She then decided to ditch the plan of giving up the child for adoption. She would to raise him alone; she wanted to have and keep the baby.

When Maxwell was born, his mother fell in love with him straight away. He was a lovely, chubby-looking baby boy always with smiles on his face, quiet and very peaceful. His mother made prostitution her full-time job. With a young baby to provide for and bills to pay, she had to earn money to keep their head above water. To make some savings, she used her one-bedroom apartment as her office to serve her customers.

Maxwell grew up seeing strange men coming and leaving his home as they pleased. On a couple of occasions as a boy of ten, he had walked into his room and seen a naked man groaning on top of his naked mother. It happened several times and there was nothing he could do about it.

At 11, he started pimping for one of her mother's customers selling cocaine and heroin to people in his community on the streets, especially the Bogota red light districts. On few occasions he was mugged by some brazen pimps with all his drugs and money forcibly taken away. On top of that, he was beaten up severely. He narrated his woes to his boss, the supplier, who merely laughed out loud and suddenly stopped and sternly ordered him to pay up his money within the next two weeks or consider himself dead.

A few days later, Maxwell scrapped his savings and bought a 12-round Lugar pistol at a discounted price from desperate owners. That evening, he dressed up and headed to the same spot and pretended to be peddling drugs. He stuffed the large brown envelope he held in his armpit with rolls of tissue paper that made it look like it contained large wads of money.

He had been there for two hours, hanging around and peddling some drugs he'd left at home the previous day, when a group of men flooded in. Maxwell could pick out the sound of a particular voice and he knew that it belonged to one of his previous attackers; but he was not expecting what happened next.

His previous attacker was with two other accomplices. The three launched at him with knives and sticks and ordered him to hand over his money and goods. It was 12 midnight, he saw it coming and quickly took few steps back, but they kept drawing closer to him. Just when they were about to get close up to him, the first two shots rang out with two men blasted in their chests as they laid on the ground bleeding and screaming in agony.

The third man tried to escape but Maxwell fired at him and narrowly missed his head. He then launched another shot and another; the men on the floor were dead instantly. Their chests were burst with blood everywhere.

He rolled them over, searched their pockets and collected all he could get from them and simply disappeared into the poorly-lit alleyway. The police in Colombia saw things like that every day and didn't seem to bother so much especially with the crimes in the red light districts. Their hands were full of unsolved cases of murder and another one made no difference.

He got home at 2am in the morning and sneaked into his bedroom. His mother was away with a client. He got rid of the clothes he had been wearing that night and wrapped up his gun and hid it nicely in a secret loft compartment. He had a good shower and returned to count his loot and got the surprise of his life: two thousand dollars! He counted again and again; he could not believe his luck because he owed the boss only one hundred and fifty dollars.

The next day, he went to his boss's home, knocked on the door and a few minutes later the door was opened by his half naked mother. Apparently, she had been with him all night. She was shocked to see her son who just walked past and called his boss. They both retired to a secret corner.

"I've got your money. Have it now and please stop seeing my mom and stop coming to my house; understand? I will not be working for you anymore. I've had enough," he added.

He sounded different and his voice was laced with authority and power. Nonetheless, the boss was happy to have his money back.

"Mom, we're going home together right now; get your clothes!" he ordered.

A few weeks later, the boss turned up in the middle of the night to see Maxwell's mom. As he was getting ready to leave, they met face to face.

"I told you to keep away from her, didn't I?" Maxwell demanded.

Shots rang out in quick succession into his belly as he stammered to reply. He fell heavily, face down on the ground and died instantly.

Maxwell had already gotten a silencer fitted to his gun so no-one heard anything; not even his mom who was away as usual. He disposed of the man's remains through his own men who worked for him.

A few weeks later, he relocated to another side of the city with his mom. He never told her anything and she never asked questions since she was used to that in her line of duty; you didn't ask clients too many questions if you wanted the deal to end well. He was able to buy a shop for his mom so she could stop prostitution. She did eventually as she could finally earn money legitimately without having to sell her body.

Maxwell owned numerous betting shops, casinos and strings of brothels across the city. There were thousands of people paying him to keep their businesses running without problems and with a couple of corrupt judges and police officers on his pay roll, he was living out his dreams.

CHAPTER TWENTY
PASSIONATE ADVENTURE

Two knocks on Catherine's window in the middle of the night got her panicking, startled, and in fear. It was 12 midnight on a Friday night; Adam was standing on the last rung of the ladder in front of her window. She inched closer to, raised her curtains for a better view and her eyes met Adam's. She became a lot calmer as he motioned her to be quiet and open the window.

She obeyed and Adam sneaked in. They both fell into each other's arms. With no words spoken, they caressed each other. Adam managed to remove his jacket amidst torrents of passionate kisses and touches. He kicked off his boots as both of them fell into the bed.

Catherine was ready to explore Adam's penis and gently held it between her lips as she sucked it gently and made Adam wriggle uncontrollably. Her left hands were doing something to his balls as she stuffed her mouth with them while cradling his penis.

Adam was halfway to heaven in ecstasy; he wriggled from side to side and could not believe his luck. His penis became so full on, stiff and turgid, all he could wish for was to transport himself into Catherine. In a flash, he quickly recovered his penis and balls from her mouth and hurriedly took off Catherine's nightie and pants with her full support. He gently parted her beautiful legs and consciously slid his rigid penis into her wet, juicy vagina.

He started off up and down, up and down, with gentle strokes gradually raising the tempo and soon kicked off with a pounding that went on for what looked like a lifetime. As Catherine kept coming up with multiple orgasms, Adam could not escape her several love bites as she struggled to stifle her screams and moans of joy. The pounding and strokes were unabated and her vagina was hotting up.

As the strokes increased in tempo, Adam jerked off in torrents like the water-spewing hose pipe of the fire brigade putting out a mighty fire from a burning mansion. With sperm flying everywhere, Catherine's vagina was filled up to the brim. Both fainted in unison as they lay on top of each other to savour the grace and beauty of consummate, voracious and ravishing sex; truly consensual for the second time in a single month.

At 5 am, Adam jumped up, dragged himself out of bed and gently woke Catherine who quietly helped him escape on tiptoe through the back door. Adam was clever enough to return the ladder to the shed and made his escape. He took the risk of returning to his flat to rest for a while and pick up clothes for a few days as he hoped to meet up with his gang to share the loot of the previous night.

CHAPTER TWENTY-ONE
THE BOOTY

The gang met up at 6am at the Red Lion near Kingston train station. They were all hooded up in black and waiting for the big boss to arrive as they religiously cradled the proceeds of the previous night. It was freezing cold, teeth gritting and chattering but everyone was determined to wait and have their share.

However, the boss was nowhere in sight. Adam got home very tired, once every two months, as he was still on the run from Johnny Klash. He found his flat in a mess; someone had paid him an unannounced visit. Everything in the room was upside down - not even the bedding and pillows were spared. He quickly knew who was responsible and vowed to exact his revenge whenever they met.

The gang members had spent almost the whole day waiting and it was getting late as the black clouds of the night were quickly gathering momentum. Suddenly, Adam appeared through the back door; everyone was shocked to see him.

"What the fuck! We've been here all day waiting," fired Steven, one of the younger members of the gang. He was like the second in Command; even Adam was wary of him because he was a nut-case with an unpredictable nature and a crazy temper that had no boundaries. He feared no one when he was angry and anyone in his way became a victim.

"Okay, now you're here; we've got to share the stuff, boss. We've got ten grand here in total - how do we divide it?" he questioned.

"Give me the loot; I'll share it out," retorted Adam.

Steven was quick to bring out the money from the dirty sack and he handed it over to Adam. They all disappeared into a corner for a while and Adam handed over some cash to each member in turn. He took half of the cash for himself and shared the rest equally among the others. Everyone seemed happy.

"We've got some idiots up there to deal with; the pub managers and the rest all come from my share, remember; and when you've blown all your money on booze and women, you'll come running to me I will be left to pick up the pieces and pay your ways. To do that, I need half of what's taken, understood?" he instructed.

"Yeah," they all chorused as everyone dispersed.

They were ten members of the gang and most of them had escaped through the net of the care system. Some were ex-convicted criminals who had left the system to fend for themselves and that was exactly what they were doing: 'Fending for themselves.'

For Adam, his re-settlement into a new flat meant he was being technically overlooked and was out of the care system radar. That made him think he was above the law.

He took three of his gang members back to his flat as he needed to take documents from his closet and was afraid of bumping into his dreaded enemy. They spotted Johnny leaving the flat; he too was on guard and their eyes met again for the first time in six months after the dreaded incident.

He soon disappeared into the crowd but the look in his blood-shot eyes sent cold shivers down Adam's spine. He immediately knew he had to up his game. Johnny had been watching him; like the Ostrich, he never forgot.

Catherine rang to meet up with Adam. After that night of passion, she was hooked and could not wait to see Adam who had ignored most of her calls due to the pressures he was facing. He fancied Catherine and might want a future with her if things worked out between them.

He answered her call and heard her voice was full of excitement. "Honey, I've been calling and calling, how are you? Are you coming again tonight? I can come to your place if you like."

Adam was shocked. "She's all mine now," he thought to himself; but the problem was that no one must know they were seeing each other. If the staff of the home got wind of their relationship, it would be dead quicker than anyone could predict. They would do anything and everything to safeguard and protect her from him. That would really break his heart; he could not let that happen so he decided to keep things close to his chest.

He decided to visit Catherine just as he did previously. That way, they could buy time to figure out what to do next. To stay afloat, he fingered his sawn-off shot gun and realised with a shock it wasn't where he kept it in his trouser pocket. He was visibly shaken as he quickly forgot all about Catherine's visit. He was consumed with safety plans for himself; a quick thought reminded him that he must have left it in a drawer in his house as he had had a shower before meeting up with his gang members.

Shocked, he realised that the bulge in Johnny's breast pocket looked like the shape of a gun and the look on his face made it all clear to him.

"I need an immediate replacement," he thought. He remembered that one of his gang members was fresh out of Wandsworth Prison. "Luke must have an answer to this," he figured.

He sent him a text message and the reply was positive. Luke was not selling but could hire it out for twenty quid a week.

"Good deal!" thundered Adam as his flagging morale was now boosted.

It was a 15-round Lugar shot pistol. He quickly took possession and planned his nocturnal visit to Catherine. The previous night of passion was unforgettable; he was not ready to throw that away. He had to keep that going and no staff or resident would stop him.

"Tonight is gonna be better and tastier," he promised himself. "Catherine's gonna beg for mercy and she's gonna love it," he reasoned.

He went to the nearest pub, The Prince of Wales, for some shots of vodka and a mixer. It was 12 midnight and Adam was half-drunk. He headed for the High Street Care Home where Dennis Arthur was still cuddling his Sony transistor radio, switching from channel to channel. Everyone appeared sleepless and in the lounge with a couple of night staff watching the late night movie.

Eddy Wisdom, the World War II veteran, was busy in the smoking room telling fibs about his adventures during his encounters with the Japs and how he had escaped capture. Patience, the African parrot, was fast asleep and would not tolerate being woken up. Angela, the retriever dog, was also half asleep. Missus, the cat, was busily purring as she slept on Muriel's lap who was also dozing in her wheelchair.

Catherine had already placed the garden ladder against her window wall, waiting endlessly for the magic comeback of Adam, her lover boy.

Adam was with his two minders who were always there for him as he made them understand his plight with Johnny Klash. They all had an uncanny sense of danger and were ever ready for gun battles, shootouts, and other emergency situations.

As soon as they got to Catherine's home, they waited a while from a distance as Adam made it to the ladder. He began to climb, the squeaky sound drew no-one's attention as it got drowned out by the sound from the T.V lounge. However, the minders still waited to ensure he had climbed safely into her room before they disappeared. They would repeat the process the next day to pick him up and fend off any possible danger.

Upstairs, Catherine could not wait. Like a panther, she pounced on Adam, tearing off his clothes as he struggled to kick off his boots, trousers and shirt all in one go. Catherine was already in her sexy, pink nightgown, which equally set Adam's mind on fire.

They were both smothering each other with kisses, touching and caresses. Catherine dived for his boxer shorts and dragged them off him as she grasped his privates. She rammed her fingers around it and guarded it into her succulent mouth. She gently stroked it with her fingers as she worked the magic on Adam's crotch; she licked and sucked, licked and sucked, gently at first, then harder and harder with a bit nibble; aggression, more aggression, as her succulent lips kept devouring Adam's turgid genitals.

Catherine sucked the lollipop like never before; the passion burning in her was beyond her comprehension. It was quaking as she gently lowered and protectively guided it into her. Adam pumped away, gently at first, then increased the strokes gradually as it built up faster and faster. As he powered on, Catherine screamed with joy; good thing the windows were double-glazed and virtually sound-proofed, so only the two of them knew the experience they savoured.

The pounding continued until Catherine began to feel twitchy around her groin and the sudden gust of orgasm that blew her mind away and the jerky sporadic movement of her entire body sent her into a momentary love paradisiac earthquake as she became still and motionless for a while.

Her body calmed down, Adam increased the frenzy as he was yet to reach climax himself. The strokes and pumping went on for another couple of minutes before he finally came down with a shattering crescendo that shook every fibre of his being. His ejaculation was so heavy it formed a mini-pool, dotted in and around Catherine's vaginal areas and the top of her abdomen as he pulled free.

The whole exercise was so juicy and so satisfying that both of them collapsed on each other and soon fell into deep sleep, forgetting all their worries and couldn't care less about anyone finding out their little secret.

Adam did not leave her room until the following night as Catherine made sure no-one entered her room for whatever reasons.

"I have come for my morning medication," she blurted to Josephine, the staff member who was on duty that morning.

"Oh, very impressive; you've come for your medication on time!" observed Josephine.

"Thanks for the compliment; I had a lovely night's sleep, that's why," Catherine pointed out.

"I think you should keep it up, if you ask me," Josephine pointed out as she dispensed the medication.

CHAPTER TWENTY-TWO
HOLIDAY IN SOMERSET

Somerset is a county in the south-west of England. It shares borders with Gloucestershire and Bristol to the north. There are many places of interest for visitors - among which are Glastonbury Tor, Glastonbury Abbey, Royal Crescent, Wookey Caves, Roman Baths, Haynes International Motor Museum, Noah's Ark Zoo Farm, The Helicopter Museum, Somerset Cricket Museum.

"Welcome to Somerset," announced Frank Priye, who had booked the residents' holiday for seven people; three staff and four residents, as the coach switched off its engine at the Bushey Cottage's disabled parking lot.

Bushey Cottage was a holiday rental property which would be their home for the next two weeks with all expenses paid by residents and care management. Jack Dennels, a 40-year-old Irishman, was the leader of the group; Frank Priye and Rosemary Jacobs were the support staff.

Dennis Arthur, Mrs. Muriel, Evelyn Normandy and Eddy Wisdom were the residents on holiday and they were full of hope and ready to enjoy the best that Somerset County had to offer.

One by one everyone alighted from the coach and zoomed off with the driver waving, "Enjoy your holiday, guys."

Those who needed help to move their stuff were supported into the cottage and everyone was shown to their room. Jack Dennels got the best room overlooking the seas. The cottage was a large, two-floor structure; it had ten bedrooms and a large lounge with a shiny, wooden floor, three bathrooms and a jacuzzi overlooking the sea at the back of the garden.

Dennis hated upstairs so he was given a spacious, ground-floor room near Evelyn Normandy. It had been a long journey and everyone was tired and after a quick dinner, everyone soon fell asleep after taking their night's medications.

The intrusive, piercing daggers of early morning sunshine through the windows ushered in the beginning of a beautiful morning offering a lot of promises. Dennis was already wide-awake by 4am - more out of excitement than any other reason. He clutched his Sony transistor radio like a drowning seaman holding his life-jacket. He appeared very peaceful, doing his own thing, as he shuffled his long-suffering radio from one frequency to another.

He also carried some bits and pieces of old shirt buttons and Coca Cola bottle tops in both hands which he never let go as had to keep his fingers busy. The other service users were well used to it and responded by simply walking away from him while staff were glad that they'd be guaranteed a trouble-free day as long as he was happy.

At 6 am everyone had their breakfast in peace and quiet. Jack Dennels was set to plan the day's itinerary after everyone had taken their medication and eaten. He had been on holiday there once or twice and knew the place like the back of his hands. He was wary of Frank Priye and was under the illusion that he had his eye on his job; he lacked confidence in himself and constantly felt threatened by the thought of losing his job to someone else.

Frank Priye was to support Dennis Arthur since they both had a good working relationship. Dennis often listened to Frank; they had a special understanding that made other staff jealous.

"You need to put on those shoes now; as you can see, Evelyn already has hers on and we are all going out soon to see what Somerset County looks like," Frank pointed out.

Dennis scurried into his room and was soon rummaging through his wardrobe for his favourite pair of trainers. He found the right shoe and had to sneak under his bed to retrieve the other where he had flung it the previous night. He wore the right foot on the left and the left on the right but was soon corrected by watchful Frank.

"No, you haven't put them on correctly; try again," Frank said pointing to his feet. This time, Dennis got it right and soon demanded his transistor radio.

Jack was a very good driver who drove the hired van for the holiday. His idea was to hire from Somerset and use it within the county as another coach was already booked for a return journey to London after the holiday.

Everyone was in the van heading to the famous Noah's Ark Zoo Farm for a look at the beautiful landscape over 110 acres of countryside; plus a children's playground. The zoo was home to over 100 species of big zoo animals such as lions, tigers and rhinos, among others. It was located at Wraxall.

"Taaga," shouted Dennis as soon as he set his eyes on a roaming, caged tiger. He quickly forgot all about the use of his transistor radio and took an interest in the animals instead as staff showed them around.

"Touch, touch, touch," murmured Dennis as he inched closer to the caged tiger, stretching his left hand; staff were on hand to stop him from drawing any closer to the enraged, prowling animal.

The outing ended with a visit to the nearest McDonalds where everyone ate their fill. Two hours later, around 20:30, everyone was back home and in their rooms. Those who could not return to their rooms immediately chose to sit in the lounge downstairs to watch the TV till sleep came to fly them away to the faraway land of slumber.

CHAPTER TWENTY-THREE

NIGHT TIME IN SOMERSET

The morning started with a bit of rainfall. What started as a minor shower of rain, ended up with mighty cats and dogs. The rooftops were rattling, singing and drumming with heavy rainfall so loud that everyone got scared. The incessant sparks and snakey bursts of thunder and lightening didn't make things any easier; everyone sat on the edge of their bed.

The brave ones retired to the T.V. lounge where Eddy was on hand to allay everyone's fears with his usual World War II hero anecdotes which he had repeated over a hundred times since he took up residence in the home. Funnily enough, people never got fed up with his stories as he had a unique way of telling them.

"Back in my day," he began, "Hitler thought he was God; we proved he wasn't! He was gonna kill everyone and control everything."

Using the back of his left hand to cover his mouth, he coughed to clear his throat and continued, "The bastard brought the world to a standstill. Everyone panicked, even the Russians and Americans. Thank God for the British and our own Winston Churchill and these other groups, yes, the Allies, we smoked the Germans to Kingdom Come. Ha! Ha!!Ha!"

With his right hand, he rubbed his fat beer belly in excitement and continued, "I lost my legs but it doesn't matter; we won the battle and Hitler disappeared. End of story!

No-one seemed much worried about the preceding rainfall and the day had run out as it was already 23:00hrs. The rain had wasted the whole day so that the outing schedule was postponed. Dennis and other residents in the T.V lounge were listening to Eddy while others were already dozing but too lazy to retire to their bedrooms until staff prompted them several times.

Mrs. Muriel beckoned to Frank as he came to administer her medication for the night. They appeared to get on well.

"What's it again?" queried Frank.

"Just going down memory lane; sit down, I want to share my early life story with you. I have never discussed it with anyone before and I think you might learn something from it.

"My grandfather's parents had nothing and owned nothing," she carried on. "His mother barely had anything for their livelihood. He died penniless and was buried by the Council in a shallow grave because no-one earned enough money to pay for a fitting burial. My dad was 14 years old, going on 15, but looked 20. When his father died, his mother couldn't look after him as she barely had enough for herself. With no friends and family, she gave up her only son, my father, to a neighbour she barely knew because they were childless.

One day, my father's newly-adoptive parents, not rich but able to afford his basic necessities, took my father to the community playground on a walk with lots of people there doing their own thing. Behind the large field was a naval army headquarters. They could see some uniformed men on the field and some others with ordinary clothes. As they moved closer to make their way to the next exit, they soon realised that a naval recruitment exercise was going on and my father went and boldly spoke to the officer in charge. He asked if he could join them and work for them in the navy.

The officer looked at him and appeared impressed by his boldness. He asked him to join them and my father became the last man to be recruited that day as they needed just one last person to complete the required recruitment number.

That action and that day changed my father's life forever and for the next couple of years, he travelled the world training with the Naval Music band. On the day of the recruitment, the officer had asked my dad, "Have you ever played in a band before?"

"Yes, Sir," he replied. "I led my local church choir band."

That amused the officer who soon warmed up to this young man who no doubt showed how much he believed in himself. Age was not a barrier as my father looked older than his years as a result of poverty and hard work at a very tender age.

My father's action changed his generation and wiped away the tears of poverty and lack in his blood-line. He later played in the Naval Band to entertain Lord Louis Mountbatten, the first Earl Mountbatten of Burma and the former Viceroy of India in those glorious days. In life, you never know where fate could lead you," advised Mrs Muriel.

The remaining days of the holidays were memorable as everyone was happy and content except for Dennis Arthur's usual noise with his Sony transistor radio. Days went by and the holiday was over. Everyone relocated to base in London at the High Street Care Home.

CHAPTER TWENTY-FOUR

SATURDAY MORNING WITH ADAM

Catherine woke up with a start; Adam was in the bathroom having a shower. It was a quiet Saturday morning and Adam had sneaked in as usual. Alan Terry met him in the corridor by chance. Adam was quick to place his index finger across his lips.

Alan knew what he meant: his last encounter with Adam had nearly cost him his life. He could still remember his neck as it dangerously hung between the cross blades of a large pair of scissors as he was pinned to the wall at the back garden of the house. He knew firsthand how dangerous

Adam could be and simply nodded to the, 'keep your mouth shut' sign.

He was very worried and prayed no one else saw him and leaked his secret to the staff and management as that might come back to haunt him if Adam thought that he had been the one to grass him up.

"I can only hope and pray that no-one else sees him; he'd already told me I could well be digging my own grave," he thought.

Catherine was not yet done. She sauntered into the bathroom to join Adam. "I can't get enough of yah," she gushed. "We can do it again right here, right now; what do you think?" she persuaded.

Adam felt the same. He was not going to back down and accept defeat even though he felt tired as they had barely slept all night. He swung her around and right into the shower. Catherine was already naked so it was not long before they hit it off once again.

It was 9am and most people were downstairs all dressed up and ready to face the day. The passion was so much that Catherine's screams of ecstasy rent the air and staff had to come running to find out if she was hurt.

Josephine, the member of staff on the early shift, kept rapping at the door; her room was ensuite with her own bathroom.

"Are you okay, Catherine?" she queried. "Yes I am okay; please go awaaaaaay!" she shouted.

Her reply led to further suspicion and a backup was called before staff forced the door open. Adam was nowhere to be found and Catherine's composure appeared very credible. To make it clear that her privacy should be respected, she wrapped herself in her large towel.

"Why were you making so much noise?" queried Josephine.

"I was just happy and I could not contain it," she responded smiling.

Everyone kept quiet. Staff were left with no choice but to let go after looking around the room and finding nothing suspicious. Confused, they all returned to the ground floor office and logged the incident.

Adam waited till Josephine left to get staff backup and slipped through the window with a yellow cord tied to the window ledge. As soon as he hit the ground, he disappeared into the overgrown flowers and bushes.

Catherine was quick to untie the cord and hid it in her cylindrical, silver toilet bin. Adam soon met up with his gang members once more as they milled around pubs and casinos, targeting the unwary and vulnerable.

CHAPTER TWENTY-FIVE

THE COUNCIL AND MADAM LOVELINE

Madam Loveline got a letter from the council housing association.

"Oh dear!" she sighed. "I hate to receive letters from this lot. Gone are the good old days when such letters bore good news. These days, not anymore; it's about kill and spoil," she coughed.

Her hands were trembling. The brown envelope fell from her hands and she struggled to pick it up.

"Can you open it for me, dear?" she beckoned Catherine.

"Yes, of course," she replied. She got a pen and slid its point through the edges to tear the envelope "Here we go," she handed the letter over to Madam Loveline.

Madame Loveline quickly scanned the letter; the title alone said it all. "I knew it!" she thundered. "I am now 86; what am I gonna do?" she queried. "They said my money has run out; that I should brace myself for a dramatic change in circumstances."

Reaching out to Mary Coulsdon, a member of staff and anybody who would listen, she continued, "They forced me to sell my house and used the proceeds to pay for my care. Only God knew how they had spent my money. All that money ran out so soon; what am I gonna do?"she lamented while throwing her hands in the air.

"Pull yourself together and look forward to the future," Mary advised.

"Which future?" Loveline retorted. "Not sure I've still got any future to look forward to. I've lived my days but I feel sorry for the future generations. See what I've got after spending my entire youthful life paying into the system. Now everything has fallen apart," she cried.

She was inconsolable. When Terry Gordon rolled in with his wheelchair, he apparently overheard what Loveline was all about and started off with his World War stories.

He began, "Calm down, dear; it could be worse. I never knew I would return home alive after that war. Hitler meant business. On September 1st, 1939 he invaded Poland. The Germans' 'Blitzkrieg' overran Belgium, the Netherlands, and France in 1940. Thank God for Winston Churchill who led us to victory in the Battle of Britain and forced

Hitler's hands to postpone his invasion plans for Great Britain.

"Instead, he went on to invade the USSR - that was code-named, 'Operation Barbarossa.' he shouted. "Whatever that meant, we all lost our social lives. Men spoke in low tones everywhere they went and everything was done in secrecy. Trust became a scarce commodity because you didn't know who was snitching on you or who was about to grass you up and get you shot.

"While you lot back home could go to sleep at night in your own beds, we in the battlefield slept in tents, trenches and in the undergrowth. Every second alive counted as a bonus. Men died daily in their hundreds; you could barely catch a wink of a sleep. We often slept with one eye closed, watching out for the enemy's strikes with the other eye.

"No one knew when the table could turn and the hunter became the hunted. Whatever you do, life is not fair; some get lucky and some get trashed. That's the way it goes. One good thing is, we could all sit down and thank God the war was over and peace reigned once again." Resting his left hand on Madam Loveline's shoulder, he mused, "Things could have turned out a lot worse; life is unfair," he concluded.

Surprisingly, this calmed Madam Loveline and she soon fell asleep and was encouraged to retire to her bedroom.

Frank Priye received a white envelope from the head office. It was a disciplinary summon regarding residents' abuse whilst on holiday in Somerset. He was accused of a catalogue of offences relating to his treatment of Dennis Arthur during the short stay. No-one knew who made the allegations and the management wasn't going to tell until the day of the summon.

Frank was to attend the meeting with one of his friends or his union representative. He had just two weeks to prepare his defence.

CHAPTER TWENTY-SIX

FATE HANGING IN THE BALANCE

Madam Loveline's health began to deteriorate. She had lost her twin sister who usually visited fortnightly. After the death of her twin sister, she was the only remaining member of her family. The preparation for the burial took a toll on Madame Loveline as her sister had never made any proper plans for her funeral; no insurance policy or money in the bank. She'd died broke and had squandered her earnings on cruises, gambling and the high life.

The millions her late husband had left for her had soon dwindled. By the end of her life, she had remortgaged her family home to maintain her lifestyle. Madam Loveline shouldered the funeral expenses and it wasn't cheap.

When it was all over, she was glad to have given her twin a fitting burial. The pneumonia she caught in the process would soon be gone, she hoped. Every member of staff and resident was invited but only a handful of them turned up. Madam Loveline struggled not to remember the letter from the Council regarding her new tenancy situation; only she knew exactly what pain she was going through.

It was soon lunchtime and everyone occupied their seats. Muriel had Missus seated on her lap. Dennis was seated in the corner very close to the door as he was usually the first to finish his food and storm out leaving his cutlery and plates for staff to clear. Catherine was seated and just about to start eating but was not the least interested in Dennis and his usual antics; she always knew much of those were for seeking her attention. She had chosen Adam and couldn't be bothered about what became of Dennis but she knew she had to play along to prevent a possible violent clash that might ensue if the truth about her relationship with Adam came out.

She had been experiencing terrible aches and rumbles in her stomach and occasional mouthfuls of saliva but even so she soon finished her lunch and took her plates to the dish washer. She then retired to the big lounge to watch TV.

Terry Gordon was busily tuning channels, trying to find his favourite music video station but to no avail. The network was poor as a result of the previous night's terrible wind damage to the antenna on the rooftop. It was a Sunday evening and the handyman was off duty.

"This will be his first job on Monday; to fix this fucking antenna!" Terry promised everyone. He was very good at snooker and had won lots of inter-house competitions.

The D-day for Frank Priye's disciplinary meeting at the head office arrived. He was ready to defend himself as his conscience told him and he hadn't done anything wrong. However, he refused to use a representative from his union; "They are all the same; protecting each other and dropping others in it because they don't belong to their group," he hinted. He, however, had begged his friend, Damian Alonso, to accompany him.

He walked into the room already filled with six members of the disciplinary panel. Frank switched on his killer smile and was quick to introduce his friend, "Damian here is my friend," he announced.

The panel members merely nodded to acknowledge his presence. Frank and Damian were ushered to the seats right in front of the panel. The hall went silent for a while and suddenly, Mrs Nancy Peckham, the Chairperson of the panel and one of the directors of the company, was the first to present the case before them and read out the offences of which Frank Priye was accused.

Among them was the claim that he had deliberately abused Mr Dennis Arthur over the two weeks holiday in Somerset by refusing to support him with taking a bath, hair care, putting on new and clean clothes so that the said resident was unkempt throughout that time. Dennis Arthur, it was said, had also suffered financial abuse.

After reading out all the charges, Mrs Peckham concluded that Mr Frank Priye had breached the policy and procedure of the company by neglecting to carry out his primary duties to the resident under his care.

Frank, however, denied all allegations and explained how, to the contrary, Dennis Arthur had been very happy throughout this period. He stated that there were no physical challenges recorded; everyone at the head office knew how challenging the resident in question could be and recording no single challenge for two weeks running had been a miracle, stated Frank.

He went further, bringing out all personal photographs he had taken with the resident during the holiday and at different locations and times with different clean clothes and comfortable shoes. He handed these to the chairperson to view and pass on to other members of the panel.

"Please tell me; does the resident in those pictures look unkempt, neglected and abused with a lack of personal care?" Frank queried.

There was a heavy silence in the room as everyone carefully looked at the beautiful holiday pictures passed around. Some were clever enough to check out the date of print of the pictures and the dates they were taken - luckily the smart camera bore all the dates and names of the locations where all the photographs were taken.

"This cannot be true! Is someone here thinking what I am thinking right now?" interjected Karen Mackintosh, the head of the human resources department.

"I think we need a break so we can deliberate on this new development. I have been in this service for two decades and have never come across anything quite like this," she observed.

Frank Priye and his friend also vacated the room for a cup of coffee and were told to reconvene in two hours for the final verdict of the case.

A few hours later, a security officer entered the room to tell them to go home and that further information would be communicated to them later in writing.

Frank Priye returned home after dropping off his friend. He entered his lonely flat and quickly ran upstairs to his bedroom, picked up some toiletries and ran a bath. He soaked himself thoroughly in the warm water with foam everywhere. He was so exhausted that he almost passed out. The sound of the whistling of the tea kettle jolted him to his feet. He had been cat napping, so he thought. He darted his eyes to the bathroom wall clock; it was 00:45hrs.

"Wow!"he screamed. He quickly dried himself with his towel, put on his pyjamas, knocked back a cup of tea and retired to bed.

The 11am alarm woke him up with a start. He rubbed his face to see more clearly; he was a bit red-eyed with fatigue. He sat up quietly but was still tired and put on his slippers and scurried down to the kitchen and up to the refrigerator looking for something to eat. He made himself some bread and butter a.

As he made his way back to his room, he could see a brown envelope in his hallway lying on the carpet. He quietly went and picked it up and went to his room to read the content.

"This letter must have just been delivered by the postman," he thought. A glance at the letter bore the company logo. "It must be from those bastards at the head office," he reasoned. "Those idiots who found it difficult to face the truth. Everyone lives in pretence to keep their jobs. No-one dares to speak the truth and rock the boat. Here a spade was never called a spade," he thought with regret as he opened the letter.

It was yet another disciplinary letter regarding a different allegation but also concerning Dennis Arthur. A couple of weeks back, loads of human faecal matter had been found deposited in Dennis' wooden top drawer. It was mixed with his underpants and very unsightly to behold. Frank had been leading the shift and was made responsible and accountable for anything that happened under his watch.

The mess had been sorted out but someone still went ahead to make an official complaint to head office and, Frank Priye's neck was once again on the chopping board.

A date was set for another hearing. The rest of the week went by quickly but sorrowfully for Frank. "They want me out of this job," he complained to Damian who tried to calm him down and encourage him to stand up for himself.

Frank Priye and his friend, Damian, met the same group on the day of the new hearing.

"I am surprised that another issue involving you and our service user, Dennis Arthur, has arisen and now in a different form," pointed out Mrs Peckham. Looking at

Frank, she queried, "What have you got to say about this new allegation?"

"Well, all I can tell you is that I knew nothing about the issue at hand. Yes, I was the shift leader on the day in question. I had seven members of staff working together with me and there was no way I could have monitored everything. I had to do the medication for every resident and that took time and patience. So I expected my team to cover the blind spot areas as it would amount to gross negligence on my part to make any medication errors which could endanger the lives of our service users.

"In any case," he continued, "my attention was not drawn to the issue by whoever discovered and reported the incident. Because of this, I suspect foul play. I have got nothing else to add. I rest my case; thanks," he concluded.

"As it stands now, you've got two major serious incidents of abuse and gross negligence of a particular resident against you and it would be unfair to let you off lightly without setting an example," Peckham replied. "I am obliged to suspend you from your duties till further notice as we carry on investigations into these serious allegations levelled against you. You are suspended from all duties with immediate effect. Go home till you hear from us; thanks for your attendance, "she concluded and the meeting came to a close and everyone dispersed.

CHAPTER TWENTY-SEVEN
A NICE CUPPA TEA

"Early breakfast of toast, a nice cuppa tea and a lovely cigarette makes the old girl giggly and a lot happier; hahaha!!" declared Madam Loveline who had been struggling with her accommodation issues as she talked to staff who kept prompting her to get her personal care done before breakfast.

"But cigarettes are not very good for you," replied Josephine.

"Oh spare me the lecture! Here they go again; nothing is ever good for me, eh? Tell you what," she continued, "this old girl has come a long, long way doing this. I don't ever miss my cigarette time. It's the most precious time in the world for me. It's kept me going and guess what? I am still here. That means I must have been doing something right all these years after all. So please, stop yapping and just let me have my lovely ciggies in peace. I can handle it. Even if I kick the bucket right now, it's no big deal. I am already 90 and have seen better days.

Trust me; not these silly budget cuts, cuts, cuts, and cuts that do nothing but deny everyone their moral rights, obligations, and values. I could die happily right now with my lovely cigarette nicely tucked in my mouth, hahaha!"

She gently motioned Josephine to leave with the wave of her left fingers.

CHAPTER TWENTY-EIGHT

GUN SHOTS AFTER RED LIONS

Adam was relieved to have met up with his gang quietly without undue attention from staff and residents of the care home. His escape had been like magic; he'd pulled a fast one and Catherine had kept calm and controlled without panicking as the staff had searched her room for a suspected intruder. She was smart enough to have dropped a rope out through her window leading to the street whilst Adam made his quick escape without detection.

She had been quick to shut the window before letting staff do the search. After the escape, Adam began to feel real emotions towards Catherine for the very first time. He was a man of few words and merely told his gang, "It was a good escape; thanks to Catherine."

While some were quietly jealous of him, others couldn't give a monkey's; all they thought about was where and how to get the next booze-and-drugs high. Money was always an issue. The last deal they had pulled resulted in the blindness of a casino member whose suitcase of money they robbed at gun point. His attempted resistance to freely let go of his suitcase led to the gun shot that blinded him with blood everywhere.

They had fled in their get-away car to the safety of their hide-out at the Brooks in Chessington where Clive Owen had inherited a small cottage from a distant uncle who used to live in Italy. He'd owned a small wine factory where Clive's mother had worked as a teenager till she retired at 70 and later died of Hepatitis C.

Clive Owen was an important member of the gang. He came up with the name, 'Poison Gang'. He was a convicted murderer who broke free from an Italian jail where he was serving a life sentence for killing his boss. He had never liked the way his boss ordered him around especially when a female member of staff was present.

So, one day after a late shift, his boss, Alan Swivel, remained in the office to catch up on his paperwork after returning back to work after a long holiday. Owen waited in the staff toilet until the last staff member had left the building. He then tip-toed to Alan Swivel's office, barged in like lightning, and with a baseball bat, hit him on the head and quickly tied him to his office chair while he was still unconscious.

He forcefully pulled down his underpants and used a pair of sewing scissors to cut off his genitals. Blood gushed out from the injury and Owen stood by and watched his boss bleed to death. He waited till the last drop of blood before quietly closing the office door behind him and going home.

The next day, the news had been all over the papers and a great man-hunt began. Six months later, Clive Owen was arrested, charged with murder, taken to court and found guilty of first degree murder despite his plea of manslaughter.

His lawyers were not able to swing it for him and he was sent down for life without parole until he had spent twenty years in prison. With most of his relatives dead and disappeared with no family contact, he remained inside, quiet and obedient, doing as he was told for five years.

He was a good boy in prison until one day he had a surprise contact from a released former inmate who helped him to nurture an escape plan. It was Owen's record that he was severely epileptic; he had always feigned being epileptic ever since he had gone to prison and had gradually mastered the tricks to make it seem real and more believable.

He once feigned a severe epilepsy and diarrhoea episode and with the help of his underworld friends, he escaped from prison as the security van conveying him to the hospital for treatment was attacked at a massive road block. The hoodlums had been able to overpower the security guards and police escorts and he had fled to the

United Kingdom under a different name and guise.

He had enmeshed himself in the maze of social care bureaucratic systems. Having changed his name and falsifying certain documents, he was one of the few that slipped through the nets of the care system without any proper background checks; It was also because the overloaded social workers and professionals were often struggling for a breath of fresh air.

It was an understatement to rate Clive Owen as a dangerous criminal; he was a loose cannon! He had shot and blinded the casino worker and robbed him of his suitcase.

"Am I the only one here who just found out he was broke?" Owen joked. He had just spoken what was on the mind of every member of the gang.

"The last deal was good but not enough as money quickly runs out these days," replied Adam.

"Wait a minute; I've got an idea," said Owen.

"Spit it out!" Adam replied.

Owen inched closer to Adam and whispered something in his ear.

"Oh yeah, I've been thinking, too," Adam replied, adding. "So when are we pulling that off?"

"I need time to figure that out and will get back to you," Owen mused.

"I am dying for a drink and a ciggie," interjected Solly Brown, a Brazilian-British member of the gang whose mother, Martha, suffered pancreatic cancer and had been bedridden for months in St. George's Hospital in central London. Solly's father was a petty burglar and his mother, a pimp, who peddled drugs for some drug barons in south London.

Solly practically grew up in the streets with little formal education but had good common sense that made up for his lack of education. He was very good with his hands and could surprise anyone with what he did. He was often hung around Argos Stores and IKEA shopping complexes, soliciting customers and telling them he was good with DIY and could put their goods together straight out of their boxes for a few quid.He barely looked at the manuals before assembling them. Some rich customers with no time on their hands often obliged and gave him a tip afterwards.

Solly earned a bit of living doing just that; he never wanted a stable job as he was too hot-tempered and wouldn't take instructions.

The last place he worked, he lasted for two weeks. He used a claw hammer to break his manager's forefingers, removing some of his fingernails and spent some time at Belmarsh Prison. He was released on parole where he developed mental illness and had since been catered for by the Mental Health Service.

He often slipped through the net from time to time; that made him a danger to the public. He regularly hung around with the Poison Gangsters and soon became a very important member by virtue of the dexterity of his handiwork. He threw knives and hardly missed his target.

The gang was at the Red Lion, having a laugh and enjoying drinks offered to them by random customers. Adam was at the snooker table doing really well in winnings. He was on his last match for one thousand pounds and was about to call it a day when the bar door swung open and Johnny Klash stormed in.

He was thirsty and only came for a quick lager; his eyes met Adam's and the look on both men's faces could melt iron. In deathly silence, the gang members all stood up to leave at once; it was an unspoken agreement as no-one wanted to draw attention and cause the cops' involvement.

Solly had a lovely maroon Jeep he had inherited from his late uncle. All the five gang members entered in a hurry and off they zoomed, heading towards the countryside of Coulsdon, south west London.

It was not long before they noticed they had company; someone had been following them and all attempt to lose him failed. The vehicle was so close that it appeared they were being tailgated. Worried, Adam decided to look closer; it was Johnny Klash. It coincided with him drawing out his colt 45. He aimed at Adam and only missed him by a whisker.

"What the fuck!" Adam barked, as he ordered his boys to meet fire with fire.

Three of the gang always carried their shotguns and sometimes pistols. It was all hell let loose; an exchange of gunfire and a car race in the remote countryside of Coulsdon. It became so fierce that out of Johnny Klash's six boys, two were hit in the shoulder by Adam's men and only one of Adam's men was battered on his right arm.

In the hail of gun battle, one of Johnny's tyres burst and he had to swerve off the road. His indomitable driving skills got them back on the road and they headed home with the battered tyre. Adam decided not to chase after the other car and finish it. He didn't want the police involved and all the drama that would follow. He would finish it his own way, he promised his gang.

Catherine kept wondering Adam's whereabouts. He had not visited as regularly as he had promised and that made her sleepless. Sometimes she talked in her sleep as she occasionally called out for Adam. The staff were lost for words as they could not see the link between them. As far as they were concerned, Catherine and Adam were neither friends nor enemies.

When Josephine had told Catherine where babies came from, the explanation had been too complicated for her understanding, and she chose to ignore it. Having seen a lady come out of Sainsbury's with a live baby in her arms, she quietly promised herself that she would save up her weekly allowance to buy her own.

Missus was sitting and purring on Catherine's lap. She lapped up the fish dinner from the tin; it must have been very tasty and comforting for her as she gently purred away without a care in the world.

Occasionally, she darted her eyes towards Madam Muriel to be sure she was watching for assurance in case Catherine turned nasty. She needed a witness because at times Catherine would deliberately pull her fur just to cause enough pain to rattle Missus.

When that happened, it was either flight or fight for Missus who would not allow anyone, not even Madam Muriel, to be nasty towards her. She often ensured that the culprit didn't get away without a scratch or a nice bite that left an enduring mark to ensure such nasty behaviour was put in check.

The retriever dog would have had volumes to say about that if she could talk. She knew not to get too close to Missus especially, if she was hungry. She nearly lost an eye the other day when she made the mistake of her life by getting caught polishing off Missus's breakfast of oatmeal porridge with warm milk. She had remained in the animal hospital for the better part of three months. Upon release, she kept completely away from Missus; like the proverbial, 'Once bitten; twice shy.'

The retriever dog kept pilfering bras and knickers anywhere she could find them. No one was spared the agony; a short trip to where she napped in the basement of the house would shock anyone who visited. People lost counts of bras and panties she turned into her mattress for a comfortable resting place. Neighbours looking for their knickers, stockings, panties, and even toothbrushes always had one thought in mind: "It must be with Angela, the retriever dog, the thieving bastard!"

On numerous occasions they were proved right. Angela barked a lot to cover her tracks and mask what she did. With time, neighbours began to warm-up to her beautiful antics and jokingly nicknamed her, 'The Thieving Bastard.' Funnily enough, she loved the name and wagged her tail each time kids in the neighbourhood shouted her new name.

Even Patience, the African parrot, could be heard shouting the name each time she saw her retrieving people's clothes to hide in her usual basement but she would never wag a tail for Patience. They never warmed up to each other like Missus did with Patience.

There had been occasions of constant harassment from the dog as she barked and chased after Patience in her cage, jumping up in desperation to steal her food even if she had finished hers minutes earlier. Patience never liked that and by the time she had settled down for friendship, the damage was already done. That was one of the reasons she tried shopping her to staff by squawking very loudly, "Thieving Bastard! Thieving Bastard!! Thieving Bastard!!!" drawing attention to the retriever's latest crime.

The funny side was, the more Patience squawked, the happier Angela looked as she increased the wagging of her tail, thinking she was being spoiled with praises for her thieving adventures and appeared to make more rounds than ever. Neighbours were beginning to lose patience as complaints kept piling up for the management to do something before things got out of hand.

All Angela could do was jump around in merriment.

New accommodation was found for Madam Loveline and a date was set for her to view and accept the offer of the place before moving in. "And what happens if I don't like the place?" she asked Katie Hobob, her social worker.

"Well, I am not sure you've got much choice as your circumstances have changed and your savings have run out. The council has been bending backwards to find funding for this place but the price hasn't added up yet. Fingers crossed; you could be lucky," she replied.

"Whatever you lot do, just remember I paid taxes all my working life in this country and now, this is all I get; just remember that!" she concluded.

She spent the entire evening talking to Patience, probably sharing her worries. A problem shared was half solved, she supposed.

Missus was seen dragging around Catherine's old brown teddy bear, trying to rip it open as if to find some hidden food inside of it. It was her favourite plaything, disused by Catherine who had replaced it with a giant snowy white woollen teddy bear; her last birthday present from Adam.

Madam Loveline was still awaiting her social worker's arrival for the final view of the new accommodation. She didn't like the idea of leaving her, old place; that was the home that suited her and where she had spent most of her jolly days. She had made lots of good friends there and it was quite unthinkable for anyone in their right mind to dream of shipping her off to a new settlement.

"The idea is both bizarre and unconscionable," she confessed to Madam Muriel who often lent a sympathetic ear and a willing shoulder to cry on; they were both retired professionals. They were still chatting when Amanda stormed into the T.V room and demanded to know whether anyone had seen Angela, new resident Catalogue Kato's dog.

A neighbour had been looking for her new baby's diaper and a blue kiddie chequered overall and they suspected the dog. Catalogue was a bit fed-up with the many complaints about Angela. He knew he had to do something very drastic before Carol, the house manager, kicked them out.

Angela was the only companion, relative, and confidant Kato had ever had as he never knew who his father was and lost his biological mother at the age of four. Ever since, he had always admired anyone who remotely resembled his late mom; not that he could recognize her but he had a couple of her photographs handed over to him by the adoption agency.

He was always protective of anyone who looked like her; especially if they were red-headed like his mom, Victoria, before she died. Kato was quick to lure Angela who was uncontrollably wagging her tail not knowing what the reason was; maybe a great meal of chicken soup or some juicy bones to crack right inside Kato's room.

He warned her secretly not to ever take people's property, especially clothing items and that if she did it again, he would give her up to the Battersea Cats and Dogs Home. That name rang a bell and Angela showed that she knew what her owner meant by the whimpering, subdued sound she made.

Kato knew his warning had hit home to Angela; whether she would promise to stop completely would be another story. In fact, the thieving did stop for some time but three weeks later, she started up again.

Jack Dennels was very pleased with Frank Priye's alternative. At least his job was safe for the moment. He would not need to work too hard as if he was constantly in a game of Russian roulette with someone.

The coast was clear and he could take liberties as much as he wanted.

Frank had already waited a couple of months and was still not called back to resume his normal duties. He registered and worked temporarily with a couple of agencies where he could do longer hours and make more money but what he could not guarantee was his pension, sick leave pay and other statutory benefits of a full-time employee.

He knew what fate awaited him as a part-time worker in some homes. A particular case he could recollect was the day he did a waking night shift in Borehamward, one of the promising homes for posh residents. What started as a nice shift ended up a nightmare with thousands of unrealistic expectations set in place by the service providers.

Borehamward was a four- floor, large building with twenty residents; five girls and four women and eight boys and three men with learning disabilities and epilepsy. The residents were lovely people but with very challenging needs. During the staff hand-over meeting, Frank asked, "How many residents do you have in this home?"

"Twenty," replied Karol Zicheal, the hand-over team leader.

"That's great; what a beautiful home!" Frank replied. "How many staff do you have for waking nights each night?" he queried.

"Just two," Karol replied.

"Two?" repeated Frank. That was when he began to feel uneasy.

Karol handed him a huge file. "This contains the policy and procedures of the home," she said, pointing to the large, grey, metal shelf in the corner of the office. She continued, "Those white rubber folders with names on them contain every piece of personal and daily information regarding each resident and how to support them," she advised.

By the wall in the office was a pink file containing night staff information. Frank was to pair up with Florentina Zulu, a South African lady, for the night shift. She looked after the girls and ladies while Frank took charge of the boys and men.

Frank picked up the waking night duty file and glanced through the chores he had to contend with for the night. He almost lost his breath; twenty residents to be checked every ten minutes in case they suffered seizures, there were dishes and ironing to be done (loads of it) he had to mop the floors, clean the gas cooker and refrigerators, plug wheelchairs into the electric mains, do the laundry, check and change pads every 10-15 minutes, tidy the kitchen, bring out the menu for the next day and defrost the meat for the next day's meal; check the fridge temperature, wipe down the chairs, mop and clean the office, clean the glass windows - the list was endless with no room for errors.

"What an unrealistic expectation from these people who should know better?" blasted Frank, as he handed the file over to Florentina Zuluto to go through; both of them were from the agencies and had never worked a shift at Borehamward before.

There were no permanent staff on hand to direct them; they had all rung in sick. It was a calculated, legal loophole of avoiding work without penalties but who could blame them?

"With this mad list, if I were in their shoes, I would do the same; bunk off work and claim sick leave with sick pay all for free. It is so easy and I would still get my full paycheque," joked Frank.

The craziest part of the job was the constant off-the-hook blazing residents' emergency alarm that kept driving everyone up the wall as someone had to investigate every alarm that went off and 9 out of 10 were false. To make matters worse, you had to swipe on the time machine every 30 minutes; that was what the bosses used to catch you out if you had been sleeping. Staff had to deal with all that and by the time they were about to settle down to do other chores, it was time to go sort out another emergency alarm.

"You jump from floor to floor but every one of them was a false alarms; a trigger could just be the raise of a finger or a sudden sneeze -and then you've got the ten-minute regular check on each resident to be signed, and recorded," lamented Frank.

By 5 o'clock in the morning, Frank and Florentina were already exhausted and red-eyed; not a wink of sleep nor a minute's break. They had been on their feet all night.

"Not sure I will work here ever again; I am cancelling all my remaining booked shifts as soon as I get home. I want to live long enough to give my daughter's hand in marriage. If I continue working here, I could drop dead before my time," Florentina blurted out.

Frank gave her a knowing look and continued with his paper work. Six months later, Borehamward Care Home appeared on the front pages of all local and national newspapers. 'A terrible case of gross negligence and institutional abuse in Borehamward Care Home that led to the death of five residents,' the story read. 'The home was shut down for good.

Investigations showed they failed to meet the standards set out by the Care Quality Standard; the body empowered to monitor care homes.'

Hell was let loose as the news travelled far and wide and all attempts by the owners to stifle the press's negative coverage fell on deaf ears as no-one could stop the already blazing fire of criticism consuming the home. Word went round that Borehamward Care Homes had earlier received several warning letters from the CQC authorities regarding many issues and was told to chip or ship out.

Six months later, a new name appeared on the same building. It was another home with same staff and few changes in management with similar services. Borehamward Home had resurrected under a new name, 'East Chessingstone Care Group Ltd,' but with the same owners and the same old habits lingering on.

CHAPTER TWENTY-NINE
SPECIAL INVITATION

It was a bright summer afternoon and Adam Slater invited Catherine to his one-bedroom flat and she agreed. It was big news in the home since nothing like that had ever happened before.

Carol Magnum was aware of the invitation and agreed to the visit but under staff supervision. She, however, secretly instructed that they be prevented from touching each other. Josephine was detailed to escort her. To everyone, Adam and Catherine were just casual friends and they assumed there was nothing serious going on between them.

Catherine and Josephine arrived on time just when Adam had returned from shopping. He wanted to prepare mashed potatoes, roast chicken, gravy and mixed vegetables. Adam had a tender side to his personality, especially in matters concerning Catherine. He took his time to mash the potatoes and added margarine and a bit of milk. The aroma of the chicken pervaded the air and in no time, dinner was served. Everyone was ecstatic and really enjoyed the food.

"Cheeky guy," puffed Josephine, "So you could cook this well and you let us do it all alone back then when you were with us."

"Well, I got the skills back in the days when mom used to be our Catholic school dinner lady; I used to do stuff for her when she was tired. So I pretty well could do some dishes. Hahaha!!!" he chuckled.

Catherine offered to wash the dishes as a thank you offer for cooking such a delicious meal. Both were aware they could not show any intimate affection for each other as they knew the hawk was watching.

She would tell it all to Carol Magnum. A few hours later, Catherine and Josephine returned home. Catherine got a little treat of two roasted chicken thighs; one for Missus and the other for Angela. She was not quite such a big fan of Patience, the African red-tailed parrot. "She's too loud for my liking," she said.

CHAPTER THIRTY

WAKEY, WAKEY, TIME FOR YOUR MEDS!

Quadri Alihu was a 24-year-old man and a non-mobile resident on the ground floor of the home; that was in the unit for clients with epilepsy and brain injuries. It was a 24-hour, round-the-clock service.

His father, Quadri Ibrahim, was a very prominent politician in the Middle East and his mother, a white British woman, who met his father twenty-four years ago when both of them were accounting students of Cambridge University. What had started as a normal friendship based on joint class tutorials went a bit further.

As time went on, Quadri Ibrahim and Elizabeth Surrey became so close that they both admired each other's talents and abilities and before anyone knew it, they had started seeing each other. One thing led to another and Elizabeth became pregnant. As a daughter of a very strict Vicar, abortion was completely out of the question when her parents found out she was pregnant.

Quadri Ibrahim Snr was from a very strict Muslim family and would not want their son to marry a non-Muslim as their faith forbade that. Both sets of parents didn't see eye to eye as they blamed each other for allowing the relationship to start in the first place. To them, their religious stance was non-negotiable. The bitterness was so much that the young lovers realised they had to do something very drastic if they wanted to remain a couple.

"I don't care about what my parents think or say; fuck the religion; fuck the faith; who cares? This is my life and my unborn baby's life; whatever anyone thinks or says is their headache, not mine," fumed Quadri. "They think the world revolves around them; no one will run my life for me. It's my life and what I want; no faith is worth denying me my happiness."

"To hell with everyone of them," Elizabeth added. "You know what; I don't plan to see any of these people any time soon. Tomorrow, we'll go to our local registry office and get married. With families like them, who needs an enemy?"

"Yes, tomorrow we will just get there with few of our course mates and get hitched,pronto!" repeated Quadri.

The days and months after were their worst nightmares as both parents washed their hands of giving them their stubborn children any financial support. They denied them funds and every other thing that could make life bearable for them. They were both in their final years with school fees, rent and food among other bills to be paid; and most importantly, preparing for the arrival of the new baby.

All that cost money so they both had to take menial jobs to make a living. Quadri got a job in a local fish and chip shop owned by a Spanish family while Elizabeth got a carer's job despite her pregnancy. She did well to hide her bump for a couple of months until it became too obvious her unborn baby's life could be at risk if she continued.

She stopped when her pregnancy was seven-and-a-half months gone. They still had to contend with the daily rigour of their lectures and studies. With no extra income, they were practically living on a shoestring. It wasn't how they thought it would turn out but there was no going back. Their minds were made up.

Even their wealthy cousins who could have helped also abandoned them in their hour of need. They barely saw eye to eye nor spoke to the couple simply because the families did not have their way.

A couple of months later, Elizabeth delivered a lovely baby boy who was named Quadri Ibrahim Alihu (Junior). Alihu was the name of his late great-grandfather, a highly revered Islamic scholar of his time. Quadri Jnr was born a normal child with an angelic face and handsome all over like his father who was a second cousin to Dennis Arthur; both sets of parents knew each other but everyone kept their distance and carried on with their lives without ever connecting.

With the passage of time, hard work, and perseverance, Quadri and Elizabeth graduated from university with good grades; they got good jobs with multinational oil exploration companies which later got them transferred to one of their main offices in the Middle East.

Quadri Alihu Jnr was 18 years old then when the family relocated to Allepo in Syria where the Exxone Oil Exploration headquarters was situated. When the Syrian war broke out, it was a quiet Sunday morning. The first few missiles fired hit the home of the Quadris and turned the beautiful edifice into rubble. Elizabeth's two daughters were buried in a huge pile of rubble while asleep in their rooms. She herself was lucky to be alive because she was on a night shift at work. Quadri Snr was able to escape with Alihu after the second missile razed half of his own bedroom.

Quadri Jnr was rounding up his school homework on his father's computer when he was hit by particles of the exploded bomb. Pieces of it got into his head and as a result, he was flown to the United Kingdom for treatment.

Quadri Jnr spent three years in hospital and underwent several operations. NHS staff did a wonderful job on him but at the end, he was left with occasional epilepsy and unsteadiness on his feet but, "he remained alive and that was what really mattered," Elizabeth often said as she mourned the untimely death of her daughters.

Quadri Jnr remained on the third floor of the home where he had lived on discharge from the hospital. Constant episodes of epilepsy made it difficult for him to be left unattended to. As a result, he needed constant support and stayed in bed most of the day.

He never liked taking his medication but staff found a way around it. He loved chocolate mousse and yoghurt so staff secretly buried his pills in a spoonful of pudding. That was the only way he took his medication with smiles and laughter.

Elizabeth took up a part-time job so she could have enough time to look after her son. His father visited as often as he could, bringing presents each time he came. The injury had left Quadri with the brain capacity and intelligence of a 5-year old even though he was 24.

Dennis Arthur often paid him a visit. They played cards and computer games together.

It was a mystery how he got to know they were relatives.

CHAPTER THIRTY-ONE

THE RECRUITMENT

Johnny Klash was seen entering through the left wing of the Red Lion. The pub was busy with lots of customers. He came with some of his henchmen who watched over him just as Adam's did. It was a Saturday summer afternoon and they'd only come to the pub for a drink, a bit of snooker and to plan on how to draft in more vulnerable young men and women into their drug peddling ring.

Their method of operating was to target and entice vulnerable youth from the care system by offering them free cigarettes, cheap booze, marijuana, cocaine and heroin among other illicit drugs. That helped to win them over before being properly introduced into the system.

Some of them were made to swear oaths of allegiance using a blood covenant. The dealers and agents were made to have an incision on their forefingers using a needle to prick them, after which they tilted the finger to allow blood to freely flow into an empty wine glass. The blood of the two parties were mixed up with a shot of vodka and shaken so they mixed up very well. Both parties were made to recite some incantations in a broken Jamaican English after which they drank the blood potion as an oath of allegiance.

At that point the parties involved never betrayed one another as a mark of unity, honour, and respect. Those groups became a perfect cover for their drug business.

"One of the major rules is not to betray the baron. All transactions must be done undercover; you betray the boss, your throat is slit ear to ear; simple as that," Johnny Klash often emphasized to the new recruits.

In the group, it was unspoken knowledge that Adam Slater was a marked man with a price on his head; dead or alive. Adam's secret visit to Catherine few days after Catherine and Josephine's visit to his apartment had been a wake-up call to both of them who knew they had to continue to act undercover if their relationship was to continue.

Catherine was surer than ever that she had truly found love for the first time in her whole life. Adam also enjoyed what he had with Catherine and would kill anyone who tried to stop him.

"Now, I don't really care any more about Johnny Klash and his silly men. All that matters is Catherine's happiness. I have never felt like this with anyone before; all my life I've been used to violence and never realised there was anything called love. I would kill for Catherine," he grimaced as his gang mates chuckled quietly in disbelief.

That night, he was escorted to Catherine's with three of his gun-carrying men who ensured his safety as he climbed through the window with the rope Catherine sent down through the window. As soon as he disappeared into the room, his gang wandered away to the other end of the road pretending to be official gas men at work in their reflective work overalls.

Catherine could not wait; she was quick to run him a warm bath and gave him a clean towel to dry himself. As soon as he dropped off the towel, she went quickly at his balls, fiddling, petting and caressing his penis before finally homing it in her mouth. Using her tongue to work the magic, in and out, in and out, gently and surely as he warmed up for business and biding his time for the moment.

The time was right as she gently pointed him in the right direction between her thighs. She moaned as he straddled her. Finding a good position, he made her scream with celestial joy as he kept thrusting, at first gently and then gradually increasing the tempo, until the change in atmosphere could only allow for a faster thrust up and down; up and down; up and down; then reaching a crescendo and a sudden burst of orgasm. It was in unison as they both blasted into the galaxy together.

CHAPTER THIRTY-TWO
BIG MISTAKE

Madam Loveline woke up with a jolt. She had been panicking ever since she got entangled in the issue of her new accommodation. All the therapy and counselling sessions had made no difference. She could still not make out any valid reasons why she was in that situation.

"With the benefit of hindsight, I should have been left in my own home and it was wrong to sell my house to fund my care; they've spent all my money and now I have been told my circumstances have changed. They shouldn't have forced me to sell my house in the first place.

"Looking back, it was a big mistake. They could have arranged for care in my own home; this whole thing is a mess. Now I can't go to sleep any more; I don't need all these worries. How am I going to cope with all this at my age?" she wept.

"Never mind, "intervened Samantha Kiddie, her care coordinator.

"We'll sort it all out for you," she pledged.

"Sort it out?" Madam Loveline queried. "Just tell me how all this mess can ever be sorted out," she shouted. "This is all just concocted to benefit some human vultures up there using policies and procedures as a cover. I give up!" she screamed even louder and was soon in a state of hysteria.

She passed out and paramedics had to be called in to revive her and she was rushed to the St. Helier's Hospital emergency wing. She appeared so weak and tired as she opened her eyes and stared blankly at Samantha Kiddie who was lost for words but was able to mask it under the hallmark of professionalism as she gently stroked Madame Loveline's grey hair starting from her forehead backwards to her shoulders; a bit of calming that seemed to be working as she remained silent, savouring the moment.

Madam Loveline remained in the observation unit as she was suffering from acute depression due to lack of sleep, worry, and loss of appetite. Not long after, she was visited by friends from the home. Amanda and Mrs. Muriel visited and came with Patience, her African red-tailed parrot. Patience was over the moon upon seeing Madam Loveline; she missed her a lot and had the chance to make up for it. She fluffed around, chirping and calling out names of other residents who couldn't visit but sent their greetings.

A signed 'Get Well' card was offered to Patience by Mrs. Muriel to be beak-given to Madam Loveline. She picked it out of Patience's beak and read it out aloud. She could see the kind words residents had sent

her; even Dennis Arthur and Adam Slater signed the card with some kind of scribble, 'Wee Mish you' Dennis wrote. Even Missus's paw-print and that of Angela, the retriever dog, were inked on the card with their names underneath each.

The card and content made Madam Loveline break a smile to everyone's joy. "At last, something made you smile today; life's not all gloom and doom. We still have to look at the brighter side despite everything," Amanda noted.

Patience was quick to chirp home a note to remind Madam Loveline that her groundnuts were running out and she could do with replenishment soon, "I heard you," Madam Loveline replied. "I will arrange for Amanda to refill your stock as soon as possible. Did you hear that?"

Patience chirped as she perched on Amanda's shoulder, looking directly at her to make sure she was correctly understood. Poor Amanda nodded in agreement.

"Thanks!" Patience chirped as she hopped back on Madam Loveline's duvet-covered chest in her hospital bed.

Seven days later, a morning duty nurse found her lifeless body on her bed. She was 91.

Her sudden death sent shockwaves across the care home and everyone was affected by the sad news of her demise. The coroner and the autopsy reports indicated medication overdose over a period of time. She had been saving up her doses of Tramadol pain killers and had accumulated over 25 tablets that she overdosed on. Some were still recovered from her crocodile purse on top of her bedside drawers.

She had left a suicide note which read, 'I lost the will to continue living in this strange place. I felt betrayed by the system that should have known better. She had signed and dated it.

Six months after her death, a group of people turned up all of a sudden, claiming they were her distant relatives and that they needed to know what she had left for them in her will. Her social worker was contacted and loads of questions asked.

It appeared the late Madam Loveline's sister had had a short affair with a naval officer in Australia which had resulted in the birth of a baby girl, Nikola, who had grown into a 40-year old woman with her own family. The news of Madame Loveline's death appeared in an Australian local newspaper and that was how they got to know about it.

The niece had never met her own mom because as soon as she had given birth to her, she had abandoned her to her father who in turn had given her up for adoption as he could not carry on his naval career while nursing a new baby.

The social worker requested for Nikola's DNA parental testing to ascertain if she was biologically related to Madam Loveline and her late sister. The result was positive and she was told all that her mom and her sister left behind was a debt of twenty thousand pounds on her re-mortgaged property. That was the last time anyone heard of Nikola and her other family members who came claiming their inheritance rights.

CHAPTER THIRTY-THREE

GOOGLE IT

Catherine had been seen browsing the internet on issues of babies, pregnancies and abortions, among other things. Since Madam Muriel showed her how to use Google to find any information she wanted, she had been at it. She was two months gone without seeing her period and panic was beginning to set in.

"I will have to see my GP next week," she told herself. "My body is not feeling well; I keep having these funny feelings. I am keeping this close to my chest."

At a Sutton Street cul-de-sac, Adam Slater and his gang were busy throwing a game of dice with money involved; winner-takes-all. That was how they spent their free time while quietly looking for their next victim.

Back at the High Street Care Home, Amanda inherited Patience, the African parrot, as entrusted by Madam Loveline before her death. She knew Amanda liked the bird a lot and had no shadow of doubt that Patience would be in good hands. Amanda thenceforth ensured that Patience had a more liberated lifestyle with a special, new, custom-made cage she had ordered that allowed Patience to fly in and out as she so desired.

Patience ruled the roost around the home. She could be seen just anywhere as she chirped along with reckless abandon. Just as she was about to calm down, she spotted Angela, the retriever dog, shuffling towards the basement with someone's red bra, ridiculously dragging along and hanging in her mouth, swinging side by side as she went.

Patience dive-bombed her and snatched the red bra from her mouth and flew up towards the sky, "Bra theft! Bra theft!!" she chirped.

The noise was endless and panic set in as it caused everyone to run out of the house to see what had happened. People burst into heavy laughter as they witnessed what was going on.

"Good on you Patience!" mocked Amanda. "Now you've finally met your match, Angela, it's time you stopped stealing stuff that doesn't belong to you!"

Still reeling from the shock of what had happened, Angela just slumped on the grass speechless and dazed. Everyone thought that would be the end of borrowing stuff that didn't belong to her.

CHAPTER THIRTY-FOUR

DR JULIE COOKE

Catherine's health was not getting any better with constant vomiting and morning sickness. Things didn't look too good. She finally decided it was time she visited her doctor. She booked her appointment on the house phone all by herself and refused to allow any staff to accompany her.

Doctor Julie Cooke carried out a couple of tests on her and finally revealed to her that she was three months pregnant. The information came as a shock despite having Googled a lot about babies and pregnancies and child care. She was quietly ecstatic.

"Does this mean I am gonna become a mom?"she queried.

"Yes!" replied the doctor, "but in your circumstance we're not too sure you can handle this. You will need a lot of support; please give me time. I need to make some notes," she added.

"Before you go any futher, I want you to know that I am having this baby no matter what!" Catherine announced.

"It's too early to say that; we need to speak with your care team first," the doctor warned.

"I'm not joking, doctor. I am keeping my baby and I don't want you to mention this to anyone yet. Remember patient confidentiality!" she added.

"Our patients' privacy is always respected and that's what the Data Protection Act expects from us and nothing less," replied her doctor. "We will work together to support you in this but take your time and think things through," she added.

"Thanks, doctor," Catherine smiled and soon made her way to the exit.

All her life, she had longed for the opportunity to be a mom. She was happy that she had listened to Amanda who told her to Google anything she needed answers to. She was glad she had found things out for herself.

"Bless Google, bless Madam Amanda!" she thought.

Her doctor's result did not come as a surprise; she had always wanted to cuddle her own live baby ever since she'd seen one at Sainsbury's. Despite her poor mental health, she had still known she wanted one of her own.

Her health was a lot better now due to her new medication. She was sure she could handle the stress of motherhood. However, she knew she needed time for everything to sink in.

Catherine was back home but refused to discuss the outcome of her doctor's appointment with anyone. The staff and residents were curious. One of the staff rang her doctor but she declined to discuss the issue because the patient hadn't given her permission to do so.

Staff got the message and decided to leave matters as they were and resolved to support Catherine.

"I need to speak to Adam straight away. He needs to know he's about to become a dad,"were the secret thoughts swimming all night long in her mind.

She needed to know where he stood in the matter. She rang him up but it kept going to his voicemail. A few hours later, her mobile phone rang and it was Adam. She rushed to pick the phone.

"Hello!"she shouted to the receiver.

"How are you, Cathy?" replied Adam. "I saw your missed calls. I hope everything is okay? I was out in town with my mates," he explained.

"I've got great news for you and bad news as well; which of them do you want to hear first?" she taunted!

"Who wants bad news? The good news first and you can stuff the bad, hahaha," he cracked.

"Okay. I am pregnant with your baby, and you're soon gonna be a dad," Catherine announced.

There was sudden silence at both ends of the line; a lot of thinking was going on. Adam had been raised a Catholic and remembered what his mom usually said. She had always wished Adam had other siblings. Since he had been taken into care, their house had been almost empty. They could have done with more children but it never happened for them; it would be an opportunity to give them the joy of another member of the family, he reasoned.

The silence at both ends was becoming very uncomfortable and someone had to break the ice.

"So I am gonna be a dad!" he screamed.

"Yes! Yes!!" replied Catherine. "I am ecstatic," she added.

"Me too," Adam agreed with wild excitement mixed with bewilderment. "You know what; I am on my way to you right now," he fired.

"What about your mates?" she queried.

"Fuck all of them; who cares!" he thundered. "I am right on my way; see you soon," he repeated and his phone went dead.

A few hours later, Adam Slater knocked on the door. A member of staff let him in and he went straight into the lounge with his wandering eyes roaming everywhere, looking for Catherine. She was quietly seated on a two-space settee in the lounge all by herself. Her handbag was on the vacant seat because she did not want anyone else to sit by her; it was reserved for Adam.

As soon as she saw him, she motioned him to occupy the seat near her as she removed her handbag to the surprise of a few people in there. Adam inched closer.

"Hello Catherine," he said with a peck on her right cheek.

"I am happy to see you," she replied as everyone looked at one another with some heading towards the exit. For most of them, Adam's presence was synonymous with problems and they were not ready to court that.

"Can we go to the back garden and talk?" Catherine hinted.

"We need our privacy," Adam agreed.

They both disappeared into the back garden and sat down close to each other on concrete slabs. Staff kept an eagle eye from a distance.

"Adam Slater! Adam Slater!! Adam Slater!!! You again?" chirped Patience, as she flew in and out of her new cage to make Adam jealous.

This went on and on until Adam dipped his hands into his pockets and offered her some peanuts to keep her quiet. It worked as she was soon busily enjoying the nuts.

"Congratulations; you are carrying my baby."

"Our baby," interjected Catherine.

"Do you know that for sure?" Adam queried.

"I became unwell a few weeks after the last time you came. I thought I could brave it but it got worse and I went to see my doctor. Tests were run on me and I was told I was three months pregnant."

"I am delighted," whispered Adam. "So we're going to be a proper family, you and me. Is that alright?" Catherine hinted.

"Yes! Yes!!" replied Adam without even giving it a second thought.

"Are we keeping the baby or not?" she fired.

"Don't be silly; of course we are," stressed Adam. "My mother will be so happy to hear this. I have longed for this all my life; a proper family and home," he remarked.

"Me, too," Catherine added. "I am so happy; I have always wanted this all my life; a real baby, not baby dolls which everyone kept offering me as Christmas presents," she pointed out. "My doctor said they will support me in whatever decision I make about this issue. That also means we have to change our lives; no more drugs, no more gang membership, no more skipping our medication and no more trouble; is that okay?" she asked as she looked Adam in the eyes and she could tell he was up for it.

"We need to be seen to be ready for this and prove we can be very responsible," she continued. "This comes with a lot of sacrifice. It's the only way this rigid system will let us keep and run our own family. I've been in the system long enough and I've also been thinking a lot about the next stage of our lives after that fateful day I got my pregnancy results. I know what a tall order this would be for both of us. I appear more stable nowadays because I don't let the staff and nurses chase me around for my medication. I take my medication regularly and it's kept me well. I want you to do same. That way, we can live reasonably just like everyone else, and probably hold down decent jobs and pay our way without recourse to public funds. This can only happen if we continue to tick the right boxes, talk the talk and walk the walk," she added.

"So what do you think?" she questioned.

"Yeah, I am gonna give it a try but I need time - lots of it - but I am in.

We're in this together; that's all I can say, really," he concluded.

"I am happy we are on the same page; thank you," she smiled affectionately, rubbing the back of his head with hers. "I still want you to think this through," she went on. Remember the social services and how lots of them will be breathing their stale breath very close to our faces as soon as this goes public. Your reputation might give them second thoughts and something to worry about. So let me know what your thoughts are by 6pm tomorrow, okay?" repeated Catherine.

"Okay," answered Adam, as he got up to leave. "I'll call you at 6pm tomorrow," he repeated as he stood up and fondled her baby bump

with his right hand; a wicked smile and a wince but in a playful way.

He disappeared for few weeks without a call or a visit to Catherine and resurfaced after three weeks a bit calm and subdued. Catherine was initially livid with him but later calmed down when she heard what he had to say.

Adam cleared his throat and began, "I really want to be part of my child's life and I am ready to do all it takes to be a good dad as you rightly said. No more skipping medication and doctor's appointments as this will keep me stable enough and there will be no more drugs, gangs and trouble with the police and definitely no more prison. We should remind each other to be on a straight and narrow path; have I answered your question?" he concluded.

"Well, time will tell," replied Catherine.

They hugged and made up. Everyone in the home only had a faint idea of what was going on as Catherine was surprisingly able to handle herself very well to the shock and amazement of staff and other residents. The confidentiality issue had worked; the only snag was Adam's regular visits which got tongues wagging once again.

Dennis had no clue what was going on but was worried that Adam kept coming around to see Catherine. Nevertheless, he walked past them, raising the volume of his transistor radio to the highest bar just to cause disruption but they simply ignored him.

Catherine kept Googling baby care, food for expectant mothers and all related websites on the subject of motherhood. She appeared empowered as she was able to find information for herself without having to rely on some busybodies who thought "they knew it all," an apparent dig at Josephine.

Carol Magnum called for an emergency meeting after word had leaked about Catherine's pregnancy which was then three-and-a-half months old. Some staff had been checking on Catherine's browsing history and were able to put two and two together; judging by her weight gain among other observations. A relevant multi-disciplinary professional group comprising her social worker, doctors, care-coordinators and a team of psychologists, among others, was summoned to find a road map to support Catherine through this critical stage.

Everyone was silently curious to know who had done it.

As the meeting kicked off, it became increasingly clear that the option on the table for Catherine was abortion; the team wanted Catherine to abort the baby so she could have her life back. That was when Adam Slater stormed into the meeting room. He had been sleepless all night rehearsing for that moment and he felt it was the time to deliver.

He started by greeting everyone. "Good afternoon and I thank everyone present here today. I understand your concerns and I also understand what it means to give others a chance to forge and plan their own future with minimal support. My lovely Catherine and I have been dating for a while and I am the father of the unborn baby. We both love children dearly and it's been our dream to have our very own and to nurture and care for him or her one day.

"We have always wanted to be parents and do a good job of it," he continued. "We want to have our own little family and, yes, we were under the care radar; the system won't let us breathe. You are all very perfect in your lives without an iota of a problem while all the difficulties were assumed to belong with us as 'patients in your care,'" he said sarcastically, "but you know what; you all are professionals and I know that you have a wealth of knowledge to support us on this journey to make our dreams come true. We are not asking for the impossible. I have been able to prove myself by doing well enough, living in my own flat and looking after myself and have not relapsed as others thought I would. If I could do that and succeed, I could do anything else. I could be a good father and husband as we are planning to take this relationship to another level and get married. Catherine will be a brilliant mother. We have agreed to remind each other to take our daily medication that will help to balance the chemicals in our systems and keep us sane and well all the time and we will never look back. So I implore you all to listen to us and do the right thing by lending your support to let us keep our baby; make us your guinea pigs. If this works (and I know it will) then you can roll this out into the system as another therapeutic way of supporting and caring for your patients and residents across England and the world as a whole.

"In the near future, Catherine and I plan to let go of benefits, get training and hold down jobs and earn our own wages to pay our way. The truth is we need the support of all of you present here today to make this happen. If you can work with us, we promise we won't let you down. Thank you all again for this meeting," he bowed his head and took his seat beside Catherine who had already reserved a seat for him. It had been their plan to do this and they both felt better.

Catherine was not done yet as she stood up and greeted everyone. She started, "I sincerely thank everyone for being here today. You have all heard from my lovely Adam and I want you all to know that we are a team and we are standing together on this one; we are not violent people and we will comply by the rules and regulations and take our medication. All we ask for is to be listened to and be treated like responsible adults who want to start their own family like anyone else.

"This is not too much to ask; you all have your little ones at home and know how it feels to be a parent. We also want to experience that joy in our own lives. Do remember we too have our human rights to family life also protected by the law just like every one of you here today and we will not stand by and let anyone or any group of people trample on that.

"With due respect, we would like your team to start working on how to create a reasonable support package in line with our present circumstances and I promise you that everything will be fine. We will pull through but I also want you to know that the issue of abortion is off the menu," she warned, "and it's not up for discussion today or ever. Thank you!"

She inched back and sat on Adam's lap, a significant public show of solidarity.

Carol Magnum was surprised as she had never seen that side of them; such bravery, tenacity, intelligence and power. She had been married to her husband for over eighteen years and they had travelled the world and done all sort of things so she could have a baby of her own but to no avail.

They had eventually had to adopt a boy and a girl after every effort failed; so she got the message and felt what they felt. She stood up to speak, looking directly at the head of the team, Dr Joe Hackman.

"Thanks for your contributions," she started. "We shall take our time and look into this matter once again. We will get back to you as soon as we're done and thank you once again for listening and for attending," she concluded and the meeting came to an end.

The professionals could not believe what had happened; to say they were gobsmacked would be an understatement. They were petrified and astonished and couldn't wait to re-unite in the safety of their offices to have a good gossip.

CHAPTER THIRTY-FIVE

GAME PLAN

Clinton Abbey did well by sticking to his avoidance plans and it was beginning to bore him; same place everyday even when he desired some fresh air. Each time he ventured outside, he had to watch his back and staff began to notice that something was not right.

During his quarterly care review, his key worker made mention of his concerns and every attempt to get to the bottom of his problems always fell through as he appeared too scared to talk about his ordeal and worse, he would open himself up for further troubles if the manager knew he had been dealing in drugs. He thought he would be better off keeping his mouth tightly shut on the issue and letting them carry on trying to figure out whatever it was on their own - he was not getting involved.

The review ended with his doctor giving him more prescriptions to ease his fear and anxiety but nothing seemed to change and he carried on as usual.

One bright summer afternoon, a fully uniformed Royal Mail postman came knocking at the door. Catherine opened; the postman wore dark glasses and had a heavy beard and brought out a large, brown envelope with, 'Clinton Abbey' written boldly on it. It had been sent recorded delivery so the addressee had to sign for collection.

Clinton rushed down as he had earlier ordered an Xbox One games console through Amazon. He was eager to collect it and quickly set it up to play as that would ease his boredom. As he came to the door, the postman was waiting with the brown package, pen and paper in his hands.

"Hello Clinton," he greeted as he inched closer to give him the pen and show him where to sign.

"Where do I sign?" asked Clinton.

"You owe me a thousand pounds for my drugs, remember? I give you two weeks to pay up or we'll be talking to your gravedigger," the postman announced as he quickly handed over the parcel and disappeared on his power bike.

It was Johnny Klash, Clinton realised, speechless and shaken up. He quickly ran back into his room in great fear to check the contents of the package. It was only two copies of folded, old Metro newspapers with a blood-soaked, white tissue neatly placed in between them.

Clinton's paranoia increased; he would not even venture out of his room and food had to be brought to him in his bedroom.

"I'll give you two weeks to pay up or I will be talking to your gravedigger," Clinton repeated, almost like a recited poetry verse and that thought wouldn't go away no matter how he tried.

"I am too young to die," he thought.

He made himself a recluse in the home and would not share his worries with anyone.

In the 80's, Maxwell Skullcracker was on holiday in Barbados where he met Johnny Klash for the first time. His then girlfriend, Juliana Bradley had secretly dated Johnny behind Maxwell's back. They both found out when they accidentally met at her doorstep to spend the night. After a heavy weekend party, it was an unannounced visit as both men never disclosed their movements to anyone, not even to an insider; they lived in secrecy.

She never returned home that night as both men had a bit of a chat in a nearby pub over coconut drink mixed with vodka. That was how the cat was let out of the bag. They both realised she had been cheating

on them. A few days later, her lacerated body was found on the beach by some holiday-makers. Someone had mutilated her body with very sharp surgical objects; probably a surgeon's scapel as the marks were horrific.

The matter was reported to the local police and the rest was history. It was a neat job well done without traces. Maxwell and Johnny heard it on the news and gave each other a wink. Juliana Bradley had paid for her sins.

The police never made any arrests as the killers left no clue; it was a professional job.

The secret remained with them as Johnny soon became one of Maxwell's drug pimps and rose through the ranks. He owed him heavily and their friendship had gone sour. Johnny had a price on his head and was on the run because he could not pay up what he owed. His only way out was to do something drastic. Maxwell was ruthless and so was Johnny; they had known each other long enough to be wary.

A few weeks later, Clinton's body was found in the middle of the road; stone-cold dead. Some gas men in uniform came into the home to do a routine check on the boiler located in his room. They showed staff their work ID and were let into the building. They went straight into Clinton's room where they immediately overpowered him and smothered his face with a chloroform-soaked flannel across his nose and face. They smuggled him through the glass windows in his room which they cut open with a special motorised equipment as other accomplices were already waiting outside on the other side to collect his body without anyone knowing.

They knew his room so well because Johnny had watched as Clinton came out to take the delivery of his package that fateful day. He also knew there was a boiler in the room because seventeen years ago, he had worked as a gas apprentice. He used to accompany his boss to the building to fix minor faults so he knew every corner of the building.

The whole operation took just ten minutes and they soon left the house by the front door as the unsuspecting staff let them out and put back the locks on the door with no clue of foul play.

That was Johnny Klash's way of reminding others not to mess with him and to pay promptly whatever money they owed him. News got around and he was able to recover most of his money but had no intention of remitting it to Maxwell.

Johnny loved power and control. Clinton's death was being dealt with by the police who had made no arrests but forensic experts were quite busy examining evidence but not much information was revealed by the police investigation team.

CHAPTER THIRTY-SIX

SELF-LOATHE

Evelyn Normandy kept having flashbacks of her encounter with her uncle who had raped her years ago and how she had stabbed him to death with her knitting needle. She had visited countless psychologists but the thoughts and flashbacks of that horrible night never left. It came to the point where she felt worthless and had lost her self-esteem. Her father's visits had become very irregular.

She liked to keep to herself but things got worse and she soon took to the red light district to meet strangers for sex, for money or drugs to get high. That seemed to be her coping mechanism and it worked better for her than the countless therapies she had undergone in the past. She loved the rough way strangers used her for sex; some even beat her up and ran away without paying what they had agreed. That made her feel even better as she felt she deserved it.

She would occasionally hang around the bus or train stations soliciting clients for sex. If they didn't have a home, she was ready to drag them to hers. She did this a few times and the night staff reported the incident to Carol Magnum who sat her down and warned her never to do such a thing again. She was referred to a psychologist but refused to attend any of the sessions.

"I've done that a hundred times already; so fuck off and leave me alone. It's my life, not yours; okay?" she shouted at Josephine.

The next day, she went missing for four days for sex and drugs with a random stranger she met at Sutton Train Station. On the third day, in the middle of the night, her man was so high on drugs that he ran into his kitchen and returned to the lounge with a kitchen knife. He attempted to stab her in the stomach while she was lying on the sofa smoking a Benson & Hedges.

Luckily she was quick to see it coming and kicked him heavily in the groin. The pain sent shockwaves around his body as he fell backwards crutching himself. She picked her handbag and fled as the main door was open. She ran for safety and waved down the first taxi cab she saw and ordered the driver to just get her out of the place;

"A murderer nearly got me," she explained as the cab sped away.

After about an hour's drive, she forced the driver to stop as the cab was slowing down. She forced open the door and made a bee line to the streets and disappeared in the cover of darkness. The driver was still at the wheel looking for a safe place to park when he realised the futility of having to chase after his escaped passenger.

That night, Evelyn Normandy slept rough at the derelict, old church house near the town centre; it was also home to five other homeless people - most of whom were drug addicts and alcoholics. No-one spoke a word to her as everyone was very careful of each other, each clutching what seemed like a small, dirty purse very close to their chest as they slept side by side without talking to one another.

She found an empty space further down the church hall and went there and made it her own place using the abandoned cardboard boxes that littered the floor. She woke up around 5pm without any personal items and still wearing the same clothes she'd had on three days earlier when she'd disappeared.

She ventured out of the church building, looked further down the road, and saw a McDonald's restaurant. She went straight into the ladies to freshen up and returned to the counter to request a double Big Mac with a drink of Pepsi Cola. She knew she had no money on her because she had forgotten her handbag in the taxi.

As soon as the food was handed over to her, she grabbed it and ran away with it as fast as she could. "I ain't got no money; I ain't got no money," she kept shouting as she ran.

The staff at McDonalds were too shocked to give chase. One bystander just went to the counter and paid her bill. That same night, Evelyn was picked up by the police because someone who recognised her picture in the newspaper's missing persons' column was among those that witnessed what had happened at McDonald's and rang the police.

A heavy search party was sent after her to the identified locations and by 9 o'clock that evening, she was found under a big lorry parked by the parking-free zone. Her white and red striped Nike trainer was sticking out as she was giving the truck driver a blow job for a fiver. Both of them were arrested and she was taken back to her residential home - and later to her doctor's for a medical check-up and rehabilitation.

It was later discovered that Evelyn Normandy had skipped her medication. She had flushed her medicine down the toilet but gave staff the impression that she had taken them. A blood test revealed everything and she had to be back from where she started with staff administering her daily medication to keep her on track.

Nevertheless, she still went out occasionally to pick up men and solicit for sex with strangers. "I am going on the pull; I will be back in a sec" was her regular slogan to staff each time she was going out.

But she was an informal resident and there was not much staff could do to dissuade her. "Just be safe," they advised.

CHAPTER THIRTY-SEVEN

JACK DENNELS

Jack Dennels couldn't care less about whatever Frank Priye was going through. As far as he was concerned, he simply wanted him to disappear.

"He was a visible threat to my job and I don't like his face. He should crawl back to wherever he came from; I don't care!" he whispered to Jacqueline Brew, his fellow accomplice.

"They all crawl in here to take our jobs. It's good we have the likes of you to fight for our corner; well done," she giggled as she disappeared to start giving out medication to all the residents.

"He's been sorted for good and he's never coming back to us again; it's a done deal," he grimaced while Jacqueline nodded with satisfaction as she pushed the medication trolley towards the hallway.

Dennis Arthur's father still found it difficult to believe what was said about Frank Priye's conduct towards his son. "That lad was my son's favourite carer; I struggle to make sense of all these allegations against him. Now tell me, how come Dennis was so close to him and how could you convince me and any member of our family that Frank would do such a terrible thing to our son? We all know our son never got close to anyone he didn't like."

He turned to look at Mariam, Dennis's mother for an answer. "Never!" she retorted. "But that gentleman has been looking after him for over ten years now.

I am very suspicious of all these things but we can't get involved," she warned. "Let the organisation do its job!"

"Well, I can't stop myself; that lad was good to my son and it's just natural to feel for him," he replied.

The cat and mouse game between Johnny Klash, Maxwell and Adam Slater got intense. They all sought each other out for revenge or money back. It was not uncommon for stray bullets to whizz past your face if you were in the company of any of them. As things stood, police had uncovered some random bodies on the alleyway which coroners were still struggling to identify.

The number of dead persons recorded kept going up. Some of these bodies had been caught in the crossfire of drug wars and police were very busy with lots of cases of unexplained deaths; the alarm bell had begun to ring.

Adam knew he would be finished if Catherine got wind of what he did. To avoid that, he had to tread carefully and mind what he said and did while in her company. They were still awaiting the feedback from the last interview with the professionals regarding Catherine's pregnancy and the way forward. He could not scupper that by getting too involved with the gangs.

All he wanted was to sit quietly and give orders without getting directly involved. His boys would do as they were told without asking too many questions.

Catherine was really doing well; better than anyone had expected. "She is concordant with her medications," Josephine observed as she reported to Carol Magnum.

"If she carries on like this, we're onto a good thing," Carol agreed.

They were still talking when Dennis barged into the office to pick up some batteries for his radio. They were quick to attend to him and dismiss him immediately as he could get up to no good when left to hang around a bit more.

"Thank you, Carol," he blurted as he took the batteries and left the office, leaving the door ajar.

The parrot was at liberty to hop around the house as she could enjoy easy access to her new cage; but she did well to keep her distance from Angela, the retriever dog, whom she often taunted, even though they occasionally shared each other's food.

She was always wary of her, "She's a nutter," she thought.

Mealtimes were the most chaotic time of the day in the home as everyone crawled out from the woodwork to fetch their plate and cutlery. Some were not trusted to handle a metal spoon so they were given plastic cutlery to avoid any near-miss accident that might ensue.

Dennis belonged to that group and so it was the best time for Angela, Patience and Misuss as they rushed to finish their own food and wander around to snap up leftovers on the floor around the dinner tables. Some people deliberately dropped chunks of their meal for them to snap up when the staff weren't looking. At times this resulted in cat fights and displays of strength with someone getting hurt. Nevertheless, it was all fun during dinner time in the home.

CHAPTER THIRTY-EIGHT

GRANDSTAND

Frank Priye and his friend, Edward, were first to arrive at the disciplinary meeting at head office. "Today is probably my last day with this company," Frank hinted.

"Just calm down, mate," Edward whispered.

They pressed the bell and a security officer was on hand to open the door and let them in. As they climbed upstairs, they could see a police car with a couple of uniformed police officers hanging around it. That jolted Frank and his mind began to race.

He turned to Edward and whispered, "What are they doing here?"

"Well, it's none of our business; the police are here to do their job and it's got nothing to do with us," Edward reassured his friend.

Two seats were offered to them at the back of the meeting room. As soon as they were seated, Carol Magnum came in, followed by other members of the senior management team especially the human resources department and members of the disciplinary panel headed by Sarah Mackintosh.

Her arrival once again got Frank disorientated as he kept shifting in his seat. Edward calmed him down as his confidence began to fade. The next to enter the room was Mr Dennis Arthur Senior, father of Dennis whose son's abuse case was on hand. He walked straight up to Frank and without saying a word, he shook his hand and that of Edward. Mrs Arthur was conspicuously absent and that added more confusion to Frank's mind.

"The father of my supposed victim shaking my hands publicly; definitely not a good sign," he murmured to Edward who was also struggling to make a sense of what had just happened.

What happened next threw Frank into even more disarray. Jack Dennels was the next person to enter the room.

"He is my sworn enemy," he confided in Edward. "I bet they brought him here to nail my coffin. I am a hundred percent sure he will testify against me. I haven't got a leg to stand on, mate; this is a classic management gang-up against me. They've closed ranks to finish me off."

"Oh! Just calm down mate!" Edward retorted.

Members of the disciplinary panel quickly took their seats and the meeting commenced. What looked like an ordinary, formal meeting room soon turned into a cinema as the windows were drawn, projectors were switched on and lights were switched off for the cameras to roll.

This sudden turn of events was a distraction to Frank who wanted everything done and dusted with so he could begin the search for another job if proceedings didn't damage his reputation and stop him from getting work in the care industry.

They watched a CCTV recording dated 1st September, 2001; the audience was silent as everyone watched. The first clip showed Dennis Arthur's empty bedroom. As the clip rolled further, there was a background voice that no-one could actually make out.

Soon, Jack Dennels entered into Dennis's room with a mischievous look on his face.

There was human excrement on the floor which he bent down and scooped up with a brown flannel. Looking sideways to be very sure no-one was looking, he rushed outside the room - possibly to carry out a further check that no-one was looking. The camera couldn't show that but the next clip showed him rushing into the room and quickly opening Dennis's wooden drawers. He then placed the excrement right inside the first drawer containing socks and underpants. He subsequently mixed everything together so the whole thing was a big mess. As he looked behind him, the camera focused on his face thus there was no denying who it was carrying out this action.

The silence in the room was deafening and Jack Dennels knew his time was up.

He tried to make an escape but he was swiftly arrested by the waiting uniformed policemen. Those present were so shocked and angry that they became speechless; even Frank burst into tears and wept like a child and couldn't fathom why someone would do such an evil thing to set up and destroy the honest worker that he was.

He had been through Hell and back those six months for nothing. Years back, Dennis Arthur Snr had watched a BBC Panorama documentary and had seen how systematic levels of abuse were carried out by some unfaithful workers and had decided to do something about it to protect his vulnerable son.

That was what had made him plant a secret CCTV camera in his son's room with the help of a professional. He had become very worried when lots of stories started flying around regarding Dennis Jnr and Frank Priye whom he had known for quite some time. He could see how good he had been with his son. Dennis Jnr never really got on with anyone but Frank seemed to be an exception. To Dennis Snr, Frank must have been doing something right. He was tired of all the negative stories and decided to check up on his hidden camera; that was when the bubble burst. He visited the head office with his findings and that was how Frank got liberated.

The outcome was so shocking and Frank was left feeling livid and angry. He wondered what decision he should make regarding what had happened to him. He decided to leave his options open and take a long holiday from it all to clear his head of the cobweb and all ruminations.

Two months later, he was back to work at the head office to hand in his resignation. He felt he would not have been given the right support by his bosses if Dennis Snr had not installed the mini CCTV camera in his son's room. Every appeal by the managers and staff to get him to change his mind about his resignation failed because his mind was already made up.

He was paid a sum of ten grand and given a gift of a golden wristwatch as a goodbye present. Jack Dennels was immediately led away from the scene by the police for questioning and was later charged with acts of perverting the course of justice on other counts. He was remanded in police custody but later bailed to appear at the magistrate's court for trial. However, the head office had summarily dismissed him from service and had reported his case to the Care Quality Commission. He might never be able to work in the care profession again.

After what had happened, Dennis Snr was over the Moon. "I am happy for you, mate," he told Frank as he put his right hand on his shoulder."I knew something was not right; no-one in the company was telling me anything about what they were putting you through. I wouldn't let an innocent man be destroyed, not after the way you showed care, love, and support to Dennis. I am so glad I kept that micro CCTV recorder in the room. Only God knows how innocent

workers like you have been damaged by the likes of these wicked people," he mused.

"I can't thank you enough, Mr Arthur; you have saved my life," Frank sobbed as they shook hands and left for Edward's car which was parked a bit further away from the usual parking lot. As they got nearer to the car, they could see a yellow piece of paper covered in a transparent, plastic bag stuck on the windscreen; it was a parking ticket.

"Oh dear, some idiots have been here!" shouted Edward. "We've got a ticket because we parked on the double yellow line," he explained.

"Never mind; I am gonna foot the bill for you," Frank answered. "It's all my fault and I would rather get a thousand tickets than get blacklisted from the job I love most in the world. It is only sixty quid, isn't it?" he asked.

"Yes, it is. Thanks," replied Edward.

Frank paid off the ticket with his credit card and they drove off to the nearest pub where they tucked into a proper, full-English lunch with pints of Budweiser.

Edward later dropped Frank off at his home and drove off to his.

"Now, that was a crazy day!" he thought.

CHAPTER THIRTY-NINE
A NEW LEAF

Adam Slater was determined to let his past go for the sake of his new life but there were complications and a million questions in his head begging for answers.

As it stood, all the boys depended on him. How would he wriggle out of his gang commitments with without making himself their target? They would be disappointed as they all practically lived off him.

Another cause for concern was how he would free himself from the ensuing war between himself and the dreaded Johnny Klash. He needed to do something but the door was closing on him.

He reasoned, "I can't lose Cathy and my unborn baby." But at the back of his mind, he knew there were no easy answers. "I will have to hang on till I figure something out," he admitted.

The outcome of the meeting with the multi-professional team went well but everyone kept pointing out that they had concerns about him and his ability to cope with the stress that came with family life. His history and track record did not help, either; he reassured them that he would change and become a better person but he could tell by the looks on their faces that they were not totally convinced.

Adam returned to his flat at 8pm to meet four of his men hanging around, waiting. They were so happy to see him and greeted him in their unique fashion.

"Only God knows how long this lot have been waiting here," he thought to himself. The excitement of seeing them soon drowned his anger and anxiety. "I have to carry on till the cloud becomes clearer," he promised himself. He was so glad they were keeping the baby and he needed to work very hard on himself to fit in or ship out.

His gang members knew something was wrong but they could not really figure out what it was as Clive Owen brought out his small bag of crack cocaine to share with the other members and they shared their cigarettes with him while they plotted against their next victim.

Adam had been in the care system long enough to understand that trust meant nothing. It was a scarce commodity in the care sector. Everybody lied to everybody to cover their backs and paperwork was everything - especially when it came to professionals dealing with clients and 'Service Users' as they called them, he thought to himself.

"They only listen to themselves and lump their decisions on us, no matter what we say or feel. This lot don't give a monkey's about us as long as their paperwork is done. They cover their backs and go with the flow but keeping an eagle eye on cost-cutting and budgets and then watch things go pear-shaped. I would not be surprised to say the least if this lot turned up tomorrow with a different story, blaming it on policy and procedures," he added, still thinking to himself as he sat alone on his toilet seat with a cigarette in his mouth trying to do a 'Number Two'.

"We have a serious battle on our hands," he thought, considering Cathy and their plans with the baby. "I can never trust this lot for a second; they could dash all our hopes in a second and cover their backs with mountains of paperwork. We are ignorant; who are we to query them? We have to tag along with them, fingers crossed, till the clouds become clearer," he mused to himself.

Seated alone in the privacy of his toilet, he kept ruminating about his future. His thoughts came to an abrupt end with the shout of his name by one of his gang members who had noticed a burst of activity across the road.

It was Johnny Klash accompanied by two of his men. Adam's gang quickly brandished their guns; no surprises as they had expected Johnny and his boys to open fire any time. As luck would have it, there was no gun fire as Johnny and his two men just walked past, pretending they had not seen them.

Adam's adrenaline rose as Johnny Klash's name was mentioned. He went straight to his holster and grabbed his Colt 45 automatic; his favourite shotgun. It was always loaded in case of an emergency. He rushed out in time to see the back of Johnny and his two men as they sped away to the motorway.

He thought to himself, "This has to stop one way or another; it's either us or them." Looking at his boys, he said, "Next time they show up like this we should put them in a coffin," he ordered as he shoved his gun back into its holster.

He lit a Benson & Hedges and blew his smoke sky high. "Some idiots!" he thundered.

The next day was Saturday and Adam's birthday; he was turning thirty but had kept it quiet and secret from Catherine. "She has her hands full and there is no need to load her with more stress," he reasoned.

Adam intended to celebrate his birthday at the City Centre Casino with his gang members and would never ever want his future wife and the mother of his unborn child to see that side of him and risk everything. However, he promised himself to keep everything wrapped up until he was able to figure out what to do next.

That night, Adam celebrated in style with all his gang members around him; booze and drugs were easily available. Adam tried staying off drugs and stopped himself drinking too much for reasons best known to him but to the shock and dismay of his wary gang members who were beginning to think he was going too soft.

They could not figure out what had mellowed their tiger of a leader but none of them dared confront him with such a silly question as they already knew what his reaction and reply would be. So they decided to be quiet and avoid the drama; he wasn't a man to mess around with.

By 2am, more than half of the gang members were dead drunk on alcohol and drugs but Adam was still quite himself; he had only had a few drinks and kept away from drugs completely. Adam kept his composure really well; he even stopped what would have been a total disaster when Kelvin Spite, one of his new gang members, threatened to shoot a fellow just because he wouldn't let him dance with his girlfriend. He pointed his shotgun to the man's head, and started counting, promising to blow off his head at the count of five if he did not order his girlfriend to dance with him.

Adam saw the trouble coming; in a flash, he knocked the gun out of Kelvin's hands and knocked him cold and flat out. Everyone thought he was dead as he landed on the ground with a terrible bang. They were shocked but happy that a gunshot hadn't been fired as that could have gotten the whole place swimming with cops and sniffer dogs and that was the last thing Adam and his gang wanted. It could have had terrible consequences for all gang members and their exploits as most of them had escaped from the radar of the care system and had gone underground to survive, getting their hands dirty robbing people and committing petty crimes. Some would be thrown right back into prison to continue their jail terms if the police got involved.

To them, life had become a vicious circle - from jail houses to secure psychiatric units up and down the country. Adam did what he did mostly because of Cathy; he didn't want anything to scupper his chances, at least not when she was due to deliver their new baby in two months. He was going to become a father for the first time in his life and he would kill to protect that if he had to, he chuckled to himself.

The following day at about 5am, Adam's mobile phone rang. He took a look at it and knew who was calling.

"Good morning, Adam," Catherine shouted as loud as she could through her receiver. "I hope you have taken your meds," she reminded him.

"Yes, I have," replied Adam.

"What are your plans for today?" she asked.

"I might be going out with my mates later today but if you need me, I'll be right over to yours," he mused.

"You come over then; your baby's kicking me mad. I think I've got a kickboxer in here. I got this kicking all night; you need to come over to calm him down," she pleaded.

"Okay, I'll be right there with you soon," Adam promised.

He was soon in the shower. "I need to clean up all the silly smells of last night's party. She mustn't find out anything," he smiled to himself as he rushed through the shower.

He cleaned up and used his favourite deodorant and sprayed on his favourite aftershave and off he went, half walking, half galloping as he rushed off in time to meet up with Catherine for the day.

CHAPTER FORTY

THE BIRTH

A few months later, with all the care support at her beck and call, Catherine gave birth to a beautiful baby girl. Everyone was over the Moon. Adam was so excited that he invited his mother to see his beautiful daughter whom he had named Lolita - Lolita Adam Slater.

Lolita was his mother's name. Tears of joy flowed freely from his mother's eyes as she was so overcome with emotion. She walked into Carol Magnum's office with a loud "Thank you" and handed her a large bunch of flowers.

For Adam's mom, it was a completely life-changing experience. Her only concern, like everyone else, was whether Adam could hold it together enough to prove everyone wrong. She knew her son, firsthand and prayed he would succeed in that one, singular thing he had ventured into with Catherine.

Catherine surprised everyone beyond expectation. She was a natural, hands-on mum. She handled her new baby as if walking on egg shells. The baby always came first; she ensured all the antenatal clinics were religiously attended and all vaccination appointments kept.

She was immediately on the phone with her paediatrician with a barrage of questions if she noticed anything untoward about Lolita. The medics were happy to assist as the entire team wanted her to succeed.

Adam was at home practically every day to play his role and lend a hand. He could be seen pushing the pram to the park, Catherine in tow, carrying a multitude of things, including a rug to spread on the grass for a family picnic.

Adam couldn't believe his luck. Both he and Catherine had been compliant with taking their medications and did not need anyone reminding them. As a result, they both functioned well, living independently.

CHAPTER FORTY-ONE

MAXWELL SKULLCRACKER

The tumult between Maxwell Skullcracker and Johnny Klash was fast reaching boiling point. It worsened significantly when Johnny failed to make a deposit into Maxwell's account despite owing him thousands of pounds in drugs sales.

In addition, he had taken delivery of a van-load of cannabis and crack cocaine for sale through his underground networks. Maxwell felt slighted and extremely angry due to Johnny's use of backdoor tactics, tricking his men into making deliveries, thus boycotting Maxwell entirely.

This had grossly increased the amount of money owed to Maxwell with no promise of ever paying it back. Maxwell had been double-crossed and as a result, a heavy price was placed on Johnny's head.

A couple of months later, two men in clean suits and dark glasses secretly followed Johnny wherever he went. Sometimes their eyes met. He was suspicious of them and wary but succeeded in losing them when necessary.

He mostly found them at the Red Lion where he often enjoyed a game of snooker and a pint or two of lager. He played for money and was very successful, often making a great deal of cash. On one occasion, he had played against one of these men and had ventured to ask a few questions.

However, the man in the suit preferred action. "Let's get on with the game, buddy," he said. His colleague was sitting at the rear of the pub wearing a large fedora and a white t-shirt, a pumpkin bizarrely emblazoned on the front. He was sitting with a beautiful blond half his age. They clearly couldn't get enough of each other; she was literally sitting on his lap, kissing and cuddling, giggling and smoking cigarettes.

She occasionally mixed and poured him a drink from the vodka and gin bottles on the table. While holding her drink with her right hand, she slid her left hand down the front of his trousers, blatantly oblivious to the other pub customers who were busily throwing darts at a board and apparently unaffected by her antics.

It was 9pm and Johnny had won the game as usual and had collected his winnings for the day; totalling five grand and a couple of pence - all of which he pocketed before retiring for the night. He never slept twice in the same hotel.

He left the pub with his two bodyguards both wearing holsters. One could tell they were carrying loaded shotguns. It did not come as a surprise to the two men following Johnny. It only made them realise their man wasn't anyone to mess around with and it would be difficult to get him alone. However, they followed his trail for twenty minutes after he left. They had been doing this for a couple of weeks so his daily routine had become clearer by the day.

That night, they checked in to the same hotel as he did, their windows overlooking his so as to monitor his movements. At 3am, they heard the sound of a car starting up in the hotel car lot. They peered cautiously through the window and could make out the figure of a man who they quickly identified as Johnny Klash; his long, untidy dreadlocks were a total giveaway.

On that occasion, he had chosen to drive alone leaving his bodyguards behind. He suddenly sensed something untoward; in his line of business he had acquired an uncanny sense of danger and knew he had to disappear and fast. As he sped out of the hotel gate, the men moved in a flash and were soon on his tail.

This time, they were well-prepared with a hired decoy; a black newspaper van which Johnny would not recognise. When he stopped briefly at a red light, they jumped from the van, rushed to his car window and pumped several bullets into his head at close range. It was too late for Johnny who was caught by surprise and totally unprepared.

Assignment accomplished, they slid open the doors of the van and wheeled out two powerful Harley Davidsons. They drenched

Johnny's car and the van with gasoline, set them ablaze and simply took off on the bikes into the darkness.

The next day, national and local newspapers were filled with headlines among which were, 'End of the Road for Dreaded Drug Baron Johnny Klash,' 'Burn in Hell Drug Kingpin' and, 'Good Riddance to Bad Rubbish – Druggie Johnny Klash'.

Maxwell Skullcracker had had his pound of flesh. Adam listened to the news flash in the quiet of his flat and jumped up in merriment. To him, it was the best news of the century. He quickly called his gang members for an emergency meeting. He had not really seen much of them since the birth of his daughter.

Everyone was seated to listen to the next deal they needed to pull. Adam cleared his throat and started, "Hello guys! As you all know, I've always been very proud of you as we've stuck together all these years. At some points in life some things have to change and nothing lasts forever. I am sorry to announce to you that today I have decided to announce my early retirement."

He was still talking over a lot of grumbling. "Before you guys lose your heads in disappointment, I have chosen to appoint Clive Owen as my replacement."

As soon as he said that, the general mood of the house became friendly once more. Adam summoned Clive and gave him a bear hug with a pat on his back, raised up his right hand and proclaimed him as the new head of the gang to the satisfaction and joy of everyone.

They all had enough respect for Clive and saw him as a very good replacement for Adam. He had a similar thick skin and the ferocity of Adam, if not more so, because he believed more in action than words. He had been able to hold the gang together when Adam was not available.

"I want to remind all of you that Johnny Klash is no more on our back; he was bumped off last night. Don't ask me who did it because I don't know but it is good riddance. I would like to invite every one of you to the Red Lion; you can have a drink on me to celebrate but no drugs. Please - seriously!" he warned, looking in Clive Owen's direction who simply nodded as everyone left for the pub to have a field day.

With Johnny Klash out of the way, Adam was able to think clearly. His concordance with his medication had gone a long way to help stabilise him. It was the same for Catherine; they could look forward to the future as a family.

Six months later, the council got them a two-bedroom bungalow located in a different borough; it was a new location and a fresh start for Adam and his family. With a roof over his head and family, Adam got himself registered for an apprenticeship as a painter and decorator. He also started driving lessons and soon passed his driving test with lots of determination after his fifth attempt.

With Catherine minding the house most of the time because of their young child, they still juggled their lives together and with their care for baby Lolita, everything appeared to be sailing well.

Lolita was two-and-a-half years old when Adam and Catherine got married; everyone who knew their struggles attended including Angela, the retriever dog, who suddenly showed up in front of all the guests with someone else's red bra and panties hanging in her mouth as she ceaselessly wagged her tail. Patience, the African Parrot, and Missus, the cat were there, too.

It was the best wedding ever; the family and friends of the couple were also in attendance. Catherine was already pregnant with their second child and little Lolita was one of the flower girls.

A short time after the wedding, Adam secured a part-time job as a painter decorator with a small company. After that, the couple set up their own small, family business, 'Adam & Catherine Slater Painting and Decorating Enterprise.' They worked together whenever they won a big contract.

CHAPTER FORTY-TWO

THE EMPIRE

Over the years, Maxwell Skullcracker had built his empire and reputation as an international drug overlord who, through his underworld connections and bribery, and, at times, brute force and violence, had sustained his reign of terror.

His ingenuity in masking the branding of his goods had made it so difficult, if not impossible, for the law enforcement agents all over the world to arrest him and his men.

Maxwell ran a mighty cargo trans-Atlantic consignment route from Colombia to other parts of the world with a massive distribution network of drugs such as crack cocaine, heroin and marijuana, among other illicit drugs. Name any drug on the planet and Maxwell's underworld network could supply it in no time.

He was so creative and dynamic in branding his goods. His latest brainchild was the use of onions. He would make a large purchase of several tons of onions. He selected the big ones, cut them in half, scooped out about 70% of the contents and put a couple of already measured and weighed bags of cocaine or any other drug inside. The top was nicely-trimmed and cleverly-positioned on top of the onion and then sealed up using a special liquid, gum or glue, which kept the onions fresh and normal. This packaging was done by experts who made it almost impossible for even the most experienced, smart sniffer dogs to detect.

Maxwell's business boomed without suspicion from the law enforcement agencies around the world. Over the years, he had had some corrupt police officers and judges on his payroll and they had often bent backwards to protect him and his shady drug empire.

For Maxwell Skullcracker, Heaven was the limit; he had perfected his life and business and there was no going back to the days of his humble beginnings.

CHAPTER FORTY-THREE
THE UNDERWORLD

Johnny Klash's death opened up countless cans of worms for the underworld. The police and Interpol across the world had been trailing him and had their radar on him. They kept watch over his numerous activities with mounting evidence and were only waiting for the final order to arrest and bring him in for questioning over several crime-related issues; from the drug-related street deaths to the unexplainable deaths of young men and women in care to petty robberies, gang violence and related shoot-outs, among other things.

When he was gunned down unexpectedly, the authorities were not too happy as that made their work even more difficult and complicated. An investigating crack team was quickly assembled to get to the bottom of it all. The CCTV recording in the last hotel he had visited and escaped from in the wee hours of the morning before he had met with his untimely death was fished out; every camera was checked and loads of suspects were called for questioning.

One of the cameras showed the stream of the likely suspects who had left the hotel minutes after Johnny Klash did. Attention was drawn to two in particular and they became the police's most wanted men. Their pictures appeared in all the newspapers and other media outlets, warning the public not to approach them; a phone number to contact the police was given if anyone sighted them.

The heat was on and Maxwell's uncanny instinct was on overdrive. "I need to sort this and fast," he murmured under his breath. He was quick to assemble his secret elimination squad to go after the two suspects. He never trusted anyone and wasn't going to start then. He believed that if those men got arrested, they might spill the beans and tell everything - warts and all. They knew all about his businesses and all Hell would break loose on him if they exposed him to the police.

He would not let that happen to him so he needed to act fast as he dispatched his killer squad to find and eliminate Koko Handsome and Quadri Pellar, his two men who had gunned down Johnny Klash.

"Get Quadri and Koko out of the way and the danger will be over for us," he instructed the squad

He had spent a lot of money on Francis and Jabala to specially train them as his bodyguards with the Israelis' Mossad group. That lot was so good; they could shoot down a flying object. Shooting flying objects and throwing knives were the only way they were allowed to practise.

As luck would have it, the police were first to get to Koko and Quadri. An early phone call by an anonymous caller gave a matching description of them. They were still wearing the same clothes as they had in the images circulated in the media. They were holed-up in a brothel with numerous call girls at their beck and call. They had withdrawn all the cash sums Maxwell had paid to them on the successful execution of Johnny Klash so they could afford to live out their dreams.

Little did they know that a price of £20k had been placed on their heads to be collected by anyone who came up with any information that led to their arrest and capture. Neither did they know that a price had also been placed on their head, dead or alive, by Maxwell after they had knocked off Johnny Klash.

The police stormed their hide-out in the early hours of the morning. They refused to surrender and there was a serious gun battle between them and the police that lasted over an hour-and-a-half. Koko was shot dead in the action but Quadri surrendered and was captured and taken into custody for questioning.

Quadri Pellar played dumb and refused to say a word for over two weeks despite every attempt by the investigating team. Finally, the crack came when one of the experienced police officers offered him leeway in the form of a plea bargain!

"Tell us all you know in exchange for your freedom or a lesser prison sentence; we'll get the judges to agree," PC Knight Anthony offered.

Pellar indicated that he wanted the agreement in writing and signed immediately before he would utter a word. He scribbled on an A4 sheet of paper he requested. The police bosses agreed and Quadri spilled the beans. He revealed everything like a drowning man who had been given a life jacket and assured of his freedom and safety. He even mentioned the onions drug disguise, the drug cargo sea route and cargo description. His disclosure was breath-taking. As one of Maxwell's inside men, he knew everything, even the secret submarine.

He had beaten Maxwell Skullcracker to it; his killer squad knew Quadri was already in the police net and gave up the hunt. They disappeared as they were too scared to pass on the bad news to their boss.

The sea consignment was already on the high seas on its way to the United Kingdom. Panic gripped Maxwell. Over the years, he had been through some strange situations and had always been able to wriggle out of them. Usually, all he had to do was to get in touch with the corrupt police officers and judges on his payroll and strike a deal. There were quite a few of them.

Some had lost their integrity as a result of being disillusioned by too many cuts by the government. They worked too hard with less pay; for some, cutting corners and taking bribes was justified after making do with poor wages. They also had the belief that they would never be caught.

With all the information gathered by the investigating crack unit, it appeared the noose was closing on their man whose long years of hidden identity had been revealed. The police were desperate to make arrests as they planned the logistics and manpower needed to carry out an effective arrest and to bring in enough evidence for successful prosecution.

A couple of military helicopters, speed boats and special weapons were deployed, ready for the action. A large number of men and women in the police and military forces and national border patrol units were brought in for the task.

The name Maxwell Skullcracker was a scary one for those who knew him. He was a daredevil who never feared death. In his line of duty, men got executed daily on his orders. He took no prisoners; once you messed up, that was it; you've got it.

This was one of the reasons his killer squad had disappeared. They knew what would happen if they turned up with a cock and bull story of missing their target. Worse still, telling him that the police got their man before they could; they both knew what his answer would be – summary execution! They had also seen bodies dumped into the Atlantic Ocean or fed to dogs several times and would never wish that on themselves.

The law enforcement agency and border patrol team were putting the finishing touches to their plans to storm Maxwell's cargo and consignments before they entered the shores of the United Kingdom. Time was running out.

On the other hand, one of Maxwell's inside men, police informant Alex Folio, had narrated everything to him. He was also an undercover police officer but on Maxwell's payroll.

Maxwell wasted no time in calling for reinforcement. He quickly flew in five hundred of his battle-tested men stationed in Colombia with his private jets so they could be on hand to fight if it ever came to that. He had vowed never to give in without a fight or bloodbath; he was ready.

Five days later, the national border patrol team were there in full uniform, guns blazing, coming down from the sky from an Apache military helicopter and making a paratrooper-style landing on Maxwell's cargo ship. One of the commanding officers with a wireless radio was seen barking orders to the occupants of the cargo ship and instructing the captain to divert the ship to the nearest harbour to anchor for a special search. He also informed the captain that they had a search warrant from the high court to search the cargo.

As the orders were being shouted, paratroopers were landing on the cargo and quickly taking positions. The more the orders were belted out, the faster the speed of the cargo ship. Maxwell had ordered his men not to oblige but to engage the assailants in gun battle.

His men were first to open fire on the patrol team and they retaliated; the mother of all battles began. Lots of men were lost on either side. The border patrol team knew what they were looking for and Maxwell also knew that Quadri Pellar had betrayed him so he banked on his luck and bravado to escape and get away by show of brute force.

The gun battle lasted for two hours with lots of casualties. The national border patrol called for reinforcement by land, air, and sea. The battle was so intense and lots of Maxwell's men were gunned down. That was when he realised the game was up; an order came from the commanding officer to bomb the cargo ship.

As the order was carried out, in the haze and confusion of great fire and smoke, Maxwell and some of his surviving men dived into the sea. As very good swimmer, he went straight to the bottom of the ship where his getaway submarine was anchored - only to see it being driven away by one of the well-trained marine border officers.

He swam very fast in the hope of catching up with the submarine but failed. Maxwell was never a man to trust anyone; he swam straight back to the rear side of the large cargo ship where he had previously secretly attached another smaller, state-of-the-art version of the same custom-made submarine to the rear side of the ship.

He was the only one who knew where it was. It was his last surprise and trump card if things ever went wrong the way - as they had. He only needed to activate the submarine using the microchip buried inside his right palm. It was his last chance; he had always known that something like this would arise where he would have to think outside the box to survive.

It had paid off, he thought. Running out of breath, he quickly activated the submarine's engine using the hidden microchip. The engine started and as he drove off in the opposite direction, he heard a massive explosion as the ship blew sky high with million fragments scattered everywhere with the acrid and pungent smell of drugs renting the air.

Maxwell only sustained some minor injuries as he headed back to Colombia in his state-of-the-art submarine with thousands of worries in his mind.

The border patrol team and the police authorities had no reason to believe he had survived the ordeal so the case was closed and Maxwell Skullcracker was still at large.

END

Lightning Source UK Ltd.
Milton Keynes UK
UKOW0 f1042250218

3 84 1UK00001B/25/P